# BLANK

## Trina St. Jean

ORCA BOOK PUBLISHERS

**Library and Archives Canada Cataloguing in Publication**

St. Jean, Trina, 1971–, author
Blank / Trina St. Jean.

Issued in print and electronic formats.
ISBN 978-1-4598-0807-2 (pbk.).—ISBN 978-1-4598-0808-9 (pdf).—
ISBN 978-1-4598-0809-6 (epub)

I. Title.
PS8637.A45724B53 2015     jc813'.6     C2014-906661-9
C2014-906662-7

First published in the United States, 2015
**Library of Congress Control Number:** 2014952054

**Summary**: Jessica struggles with retrograde amnesia after she is injured
by a bison on her family's ranch.

*Orca Book Publishers is dedicated to preserving the environment and has
printed this book on Forest Stewardship Council® certified paper.*

Orca Book Publishers gratefully acknowledges the support for its publishing
programs provided by the following agencies: the Government of Canada through
the Canada Book Fund and the Canada Council for the Arts, and the Province of British
Columbia through the BC Arts Council and the Book Publishing Tax Credit.

Cover design by Chantal Gabriell
Cover images by Getty Images
Author photo by Eileen Abad

ORCA BOOK PUBLISHERS
PO Box 5626, Stn. B
Victoria, BC  Canada
V8R 6S4

ORCA BOOK PUBLISHERS
PO Box 468
Custer, WA  USA
98240-0468

www.orcabook.com
Printed and bound in Canada.

18  17  16  15  •  4  3  2  1

*To my daughters, Anissa and Elianne.*
*I love you both to infinity and back.*

# Part I:

## AWAKE

*Each day is a little life:*
*every waking and rising a little birth,*
*every fresh morning a little youth,*
*every going to rest and sleep a little death.*

—Arthur Schopenhauer
*The Essays of Arthur Schopenhauer; Counsels and Maxims*

# Snapshots

I remember.

That's what they want me to say, this Woman sitting beside my bed, this Man by the window. But I won't, because it would be a lie.

The Woman places a stack of photos on my bedside table, then slowly slides the top one toward me. Her eyes dart from me to the Man. He leans against the wall by the window, staring at the tree branches outside.

"Honey," she calls to him, her voice tight. He looks at us over his shoulder with tired eyes, then shuffles closer. It feels like the room, the entire building maybe, sucks in its breath when I pick up the photo and study it carefully, slowly, as if my life depended on it. Because it kind of does.

A family stands on the beach. The Woman, petite with wavy black hair, has her arms around the Girl's shoulders. The Girl's sunburned face is lit up by a grin. The Boy, wearing an oversized pirate hat, sits on the Man's shoulders.

They are all wearing colorful beachwear. The Man is stocky, with a buzz cut, and has socks on with his sandals. There are palm trees and ocean waves behind the family. Obviously, it's a vacation shot, taken somewhere far from here. How do I know?

Some things—the big stuff—I am sure of. Like, I do not live in a tropical place, and the Earth goes around the sun. It's the not-so-minor details that leave me guessing, like what my favorite flavor of ice cream is, why my head hurts and who I am exactly.

Nine days have gone by, they say, since I awoke from the Big Sleep. *The coma.* I stare at the photo, the expectation so thick in the air that I can almost taste it. This Woman and this Man want my eyes to open wide and a loud *click* to go off somewhere in my brain. For me to say, "Oh yes, of course, how could I forget that amazing day?"

But it doesn't happen.

I do know that the Girl on the beach, with the naïve I've-got-my-whole-life-ahead-of-me grin, is the same Girl who gazes back at me from the bathroom mirror. But I could be looking at a photo of some random generic, happy family in a resort brochure, because I feel only a cool emptiness when I gaze down at them.

I slide the photo back across the table, look up at the Woman and shrug. She nods her head and says softly, "Okay, okay," but her eyes glisten with disappointment.

This Woman, you see, is my mother. This Man is my father. The Boy in the photo is my ten-year-old brother, Stephen. My name is Jessica, and I am fifteen years old. And thanks to a bison bull named Ramses on their—*our*—ranch, my brain is mush. One Very Bad Day, April 26, to be exact, Ramses charged me, putting me in the coma. Eleven days *in* the coma plus nine days *out* equals twenty days in the hospital so far. I can walk and talk and eat and don't need sponge baths anymore.

But my old life is a long blank that my brain no longer fills in for me.

I know all of this because they explained it to me, slowly and gently, with concern in their eyes. Intellectually, I can understand. Inside, though, where it really counts, I can't feel any of it. When she—the Woman, my mother—reaches toward me and wraps her arms around me, it's like I am being hugged by a complete stranger waiting in front of me at the grocery-store checkout. Not an ounce of warmth or love flows through me. Not even sadness.

The Woman releases me from her grip, then picks up the photos with shaking hands. She doesn't want me to see her face, I think, because she walks over to a bulletin board on the wall near the window and carefully starts putting the photos up, one by one, with push pins.

The Man steps closer and puts his hand on my shoulder. I flinch. "Well," he says, "maybe next time."

I watch the Woman as the Man paces around the room, glancing out the window every now and then. I am a lump, sitting there. Feeling nothing and saying nothing.

I may finally be awake, but I am hollow.

When I am alone and the hallway outside my door is quiet, I step slowly, carefully, into the bathroom. My hands fumble in the darkness until they find the switch. The fluorescent lighting hums, and the Girl is in front of me. The Girl in the Mirror.

"Jessica," I whisper.

Her brow is slightly furrowed, and her gray-blue eyes stare coldly back at me. She's a serious girl, it seems. Her face is pale, but maybe that's from being cooped up in a hospital for weeks. A few freckles are scattered across her cheeks, and there are faint patches of purple and green, leftover bruises from her Very Bad Day. Her hair is mousy brown and medium length, mostly, except for a patch above her right ear that has been shaved. I run my hands back and forth over the stubble until my fingertips find the small circular dent. This, I've been told, is where a tube was inserted through my skull. I lower my hands to the edge of the sink and lean closer.

The Girl's mouth opens, stretching wide until I can see a lumpy, off-white filling in one of her back teeth. My face muscles begin to ache, so I close my mouth and force a grin. What made the Girl smile? Did the corners of her lips curl up easily and quickly at the slightest joke or a greeting from a passing stranger? Or maybe her smile was reserved for those she loved, those who had earned her trust.

The smirk slips away and I close my eyes, then slowly reopen them. Her pupils shrink, then expand, but the eyes reveal little emotion. A thought slides into my mind: *the eyes are the windows to the soul*. I get as close to her as I can, until my breath leaves vapor on the glass, and I peer harder into those eyes. I see the dark outer edge, the blue flecks, thin red veins on the whites of her eyes. The soul, however, is nowhere to be found.

I move on to her forehead. Fairly high, with a small widow's peak in her hairline. Turning sideways, I inspect an ear—small, with two piercings—and then lean back to take in the overall shape of her skull. The house of the brain. I lift my hand slowly and tap on the side of her head with my knuckles.

"Hello," I say. "Anyone home?"

The Girl in the Mirror gazes back at me, her expression vacant. I know someone is in there, hiding in the darkest corners of that mind. She was a real person once, before her slate was wiped clean. I knock again, this time hard enough that a slight ache throbs in my temple.

"I said, anyone home?"

She doesn't flinch. A wave of irritation washes over me, and my fist becomes tighter, until my fingernails cut sharply into my palm. I knock again on my temple, and again…until the fist flies out in front of me before I can stop it or think about how stupid I am being.

*Crack.* The sound of bone against glass. Pain shoots down into my hand, then to my wrist. I step back. The Girl in the Mirror has raised eyebrows, an open mouth. She is obviously shocked.

At least I know she's paying attention.

# It's a Bird,
# It's a Plane...

I have hardly slept, but it must be morning because a woman comes in with a cart and gives me a tray.

"Good morning, Sunshine," she says. When she's gone I open the lid and inspect the pancakes. They are limp and the color of cardboard. I am deciding whether I can force myself to take a bite when I hear someone clear his throat.

A short man with black hair and a salt-and-pepper beard stands in the doorway. His hands are in the pockets of his khaki pants, like he's going for a stroll in the park. The sure way he walks and the confidence in his smile both scream "doctor," but not in an arrogant way. I surprise myself by knowing his name: Dr. Lavoie. And I remember what the Man and Woman told me: this man saved my life. He is a hero, my very own Super Doc.

"Hi, Jessica," he says. "Your parents are meeting me here in a bit, but I was in the neighborhood and thought I'd pop by early. Okay if I interrupt your breakfast?"

I nod, replacing the lid on the pancakes. "I would be forever grateful," I say. He smiles and steps into my room, pausing to look at the photos on the bulletin board: the beach vacation, the Girl holding a newborn baby boy, the Girl wearing a giant cowboy hat. There are also cards signed *Get Well Soon* and *Lots of Love xoxoxo*. Super Doc stands with his hands on his hips, moving his head slowly from side to side as he works his way down the rows of photos.

"Hmm," he says. "Hmm."

Warmth rises into my face. He has probably poked and prodded me all over, this doctor. But his looking at the pictures feels more intimate somehow.

"I was a happy camper, wasn't I?" I say, wanting more than anything for him to stop *hmm*ing and staring. He turns and gives me a gentle, even smile.

"I especially like the one with the cowboy hat." He waits to see what I will say. Maybe he hopes he will catch me off guard, that I will reveal some hint of a memory or some preference for another picture. I laugh too loudly instead.

"I guess I had bad taste too."

"You have something against Western wear?" He winks as he pulls a pen out of the front pocket of his blue-striped shirt.

"I'm not sure," I answer.

He nods and sits down on the chair next to my bed. "I thought it was time we had a little chat."

I suddenly feel stupid that I'm wearing Hello Kitty pajamas. He's waiting for me to give him the thumbs-up, I guess, so I say, "All right."

"You seem to be doing well."

Well? If that's another way of saying screwed in the head, maybe. I meet his gaze and am trying to think of the best way to correct him when the Woman bursts into the room. Her hair is messy, but she pats it down.

"Sorry," she says. "Ray had a bit of trouble with the tractor this morning, but he got it going and here we are." I don't see any "we," only her, but the Man must be close behind.

Super Doc laughs politely and stands to shake her hand.

"Glad you made it." He gestures to the chair, and she sits down as the Man strolls in.

Friendly handshakes between the men, and we settle down to business. I sit on the bed and we talk about my Brain. The Accident. My Life.

Super Doc is amazingly positive and has nothing but good things to say. I am strong, he says, and young, and that has allowed my brain to heal quickly. Although my walking is a bit shaky at the moment, it won't be long before it is back to normal. "It's amazing, Jessica, how far you've come in the past three weeks. The human brain's ability to recover from trauma never ceases to astound me."

"Uh, thanks," I say.

The Woman's eyes are shiny and proud, like I've won a spelling bee.

The Man's face, however, is solemn. He leans forward. "So," he says, "when is she going to start remembering things?"

Super Doc doesn't miss a beat. "That was what I wanted to talk about next."

The joy on the Woman's face fades. Super Doc turns to me then, and his brown eyes are warm and kind. "Everything I've said is true. You are bouncing back remarkably well, Jessica. Most people with this kind of injury eventually recover the majority of their memories. But I can't lie. There's no real way of knowing yet, and no guarantees."

I keep my eyes down, studying my hands, and though I probably should be upset or worried, I feel strangely numb. My post-traumatic brain struggles to absorb what he has said. Most people get their memories back. Not all. And, of course, Super Doc wouldn't lie. I want to ask him if having no feelings is usual too, but that would only add to the Man's and Woman's stress.

"For now, Jessica should continue with her rehabilitation," Super Doc says. "We'll do another CT scan soon and take it from there. Feel free to ask me questions anytime."

Suddenly they are all standing up and exchanging handshakes. "Thank you," the Woman says. Her face is as white as my bedsheet.

Super Doc reaches over and gives my knee a squeeze, then heads toward the door. I nearly grab his arm, beg him to stay and save me again, get me out of this mess for good. But I am a wimp and watch him go.

"Oh, Jess," the Man says softly, his arm going around my shoulder. "It's going to be okay."

My mouth answers without my brain's permission. "And how do you know?"

I'm not sure whether the flash in his eyes is hurt or just plain worry, but either way, I disgust myself.

# Mirage

I'm putting the lid over the untouched shepherd's pie the hospital calls dinner when the Woman walks in. A kid with reddish hair and blue-framed glasses trails in behind her. It's the Boy, my brother from the photos. He carries a bright-red gift bag with orange tissue paper flaring out of the top like it's caught fire.

"Stephen missed school this afternoon to come see you," the Woman—Mother, I remind myself—says. "He couldn't wait to give you an extra-special gift." The Boy peers at me over the top of his glasses.

My brain surprises me with what must be the kid's nickname—Little Man—but I don't know if Jessica was the only one to call him that. I'm also surprised by my urge to reach over and tousle his hair. He looks skittish, though, and I don't want to scare him.

Mother glances at the door. "Jessie, is it all right if I leave the two of you alone for a few minutes? I need to go fill out a form."

"Does he bite?" I ask, and the Boy's mouth curls up a bit in the corners. Mother looks at him worriedly, but he gives her a nod, and she heads out the door. The Boy and I are quiet for a moment, looking at each other.

"Hi, Little Man," I say.

He lets out a sigh and pushes his glasses up the bridge of his nose. "This is good. I'm happy you're awake. I was"—his voice cracks—"I was scared I might never talk to you again." His hunched shoulders make him appear small and fragile, like if I sneeze too hard the breeze might knock him over.

"Well," I say, "here I am."

He looks me over carefully, as though he's having a hard time believing I'm really sitting there talking to him.

"I wish," he says, so softly it's almost a whisper, "I wish this hadn't happened. I wish—"

"Don't worry about me," I interrupt. "I'm as good as new. Even got a cool haircut."

The intensity in his gray-blue eyes, the same color and shape as the Girl's, is startling. As we look at each other, the room so quiet I can hear my own breathing, the weight of everything that's been happening to me— the medical tests and jargon, rehab, the Man and Woman with all their photos—presses down on me suddenly.

The air feels hot and stuffy, and I can't take it—one more heavy moment and I will come undone. I let out a long breath.

"Do you think," I say slowly, unsure of the right words to convince a ten-year-old, "we can pretend none of that ever happened? Maybe agree not to talk about it? You know, just hang out?"

The Boy bites his bottom lip, his hands clenched tightly on the handle of the gift bag. He's struggling to keep his composure—it shows on his face—but I'm not in any state to guess what's going through his mind.

"And can I have my gift already?" I say.

It takes a few seconds, but then the tiniest sliver of a smile grows, until his face is transformed by a huge grin. He looks as relieved as I feel. "It's a deal," he says, handing me the gift bag.

I reach into the tissue paper, and my fingers find something strangely lumpy. I pull it out and turn it over in my hands. It's a kind of rock, the color of caramel, only it has these ridges all around it, like a flower burst into bloom.

"Do you like it?" Stephen says.

I nod. I have no idea what it is, but maybe I'm supposed to.

He sits beside me on the bed. "It's a sand rose. All the way from the Sahara desert. I didn't go there to get it, of course." He grins. "I bought it in a rock shop."

"It's nice," I say.

He glances at me to check if I understand the meaning of his gift. When he sees that I don't, though, he doesn't seem disappointed.

"Sometimes," he explains, "we go on adventures. One of our favorites is the Sahara caravan. We ride pretend camels and eat our lunch in blanket tents that we make in the living room. We even have a real dried-up scorpion."

An image flashes in my mind of a room transformed into a massive, colorful tent. I can't tell if it's a real memory or only my imagination, but I feel a tingle down my spine.

He points at the rock. "It's a kind of crystal that forms in the desert, from the evaporation of a salt basin or erosion from the wind. It's supposed to bring good luck."

I run my fingers over the ridges that form the petals. That a clump of tiny sand and salt granules could come together and form something so beautiful, so complex, amazes me. I put it on my bedside table.

"Thanks," I say. "It's cool."

We share a silence.

"This is great," he says. "That you're getting back to normal."

A jolt goes through me. Normal? If this is normal, I'm doomed. "You really think so?"

He shoots a look at the door, realizing he's said something he shouldn't have. "You don't remember the last time I was here to see you?"

The question irritates me, but he's only a kid, so I let it go. "I have issues with that, apparently."

He looks at me intently for a few seconds, then sucks in his breath. "I was here with Mom and Dad the night you came out of the coma. But you were"—he pauses, chewing his bottom lip—"nuts. You acted like you were drunk or something. You could barely walk, and you didn't make any sense when you talked. You even punched Mom."

I actually hit the Woman? You'd think I'd remember something like that. Strangely, though, that's not the part that bothers me. It dawns on me that everyone knows more about me than I do.

"Did I hit her hard?"

Stephen shakes his head, his hair falling forward. "Nah. No offense, but it was kind of a girly punch. Dad jumped in and stopped you. The nurses did have to tie you to the bed after though. And Mom and Dad didn't let me come back and see you until today."

Tie me to the bed? Like some kind of raving lunatic? I'm nauseated all of a sudden, and I stand up, gripping the bed railing.

"I have to go to the bathroom," I say, but it's too late. The vomit rises in my throat, and all I can do when it comes gushing out is open my hand and try to catch it.

Stephen leaps from the bed, eyes wide, and clutches at the box of Kleenex on my nightstand. The box tumbles to the floor, and he scrambles to pull out a handful of tissues. When he hands them to me, he can't look me in the eye.

"Man, Jess," he says, "that's gross!"

I laugh, my nose making a snorting noise that makes me laugh again. "Yeah," I answer, "it is."

He laughs too, but there's a nervous edge to it. My sister, he must be thinking, is completely hopeless.

Mother walks in and calls for someone to deal with my mess while I wash up in the bathroom. Once Mother and Little Man are gone, I stretch out on the bed and pull the covers over my head. I close my eyes, and the golden sands of the Sahara stretch out before me in every direction. The orange ball of a sun hovers over the horizon, and sand dunes cast rippled shadows. Stephen appears by my side, and when he turns toward me he gives me a long, slow wink.

# Squeezing Water from a Stone

S o what *do* I remember?

I decide to work on that. The halls are quiet and I am alone in my room; my lunch tray is gone. I crank up my bed, lean back, pull the blankets up to my chin and close my eyes tight.

I was an honor student in school, I've been told. So I'm not a moron, or at least I wasn't. A little effort, and I should be able to get my brain to cooperate. Deep breaths. I listen to my breathing, trying to block out the sounds of squeaking nurses' shoes and carts in the hallway. You can do this, I tell myself. You can find yourself again.

I start by going over the few moments I remember in the first days after waking up from my Big Sleep.

*Sitting up, head pounding and room spinning. A glass of water. Chugging it down so fast I nearly choke, my head as heavy as concrete. "Wow," a soft voice says. "Call her parents."*

*A nurse with a gap between her front teeth offering me a huge blue pill in her outstretched palm. "Come on now," she says. "Don't fight me on this one."*

*The Woman—my mother—leaning forward in the armchair to rest her head on the edge of my bed, a shudder going though her body.*

*The Girl in the Mirror, staring back at me with scared eyes. I stick my tongue out at her, and she does it back.*

I flip onto my side, open my eyes and stare at the beige wall. These memories are not what I am after. They don't matter. It's the ones before I came to this place, the ones before Ramses decided my skull was a toy for his amusement, that I need to get to somehow. I bury my face deeper into the pillow and pull the blankets over my head. I imagine the white of the sheet as a movie screen, waiting for my mind to project its images. The warmth of my breath bounces back at me, and my eyes grow heavy, but I keep them half open and let the fragments slip into my mind.

*A loud siren, and a rumbling feeling under my back. Someone squeezes my hand and tells me to hang on. "I'm sorry," I try to say, but something covers my mouth and no one hears me.*

*On my back again, a feeling like I am floating. Distorted voices come from above, and a force pulls at me, tugging me down deeper. I try to scream, to tell the voices I am here, to save me, but it is stronger than I am. I let it take me.*

*"Please don't leave us," the voice says. "You've got to fight, Jessica." A warm hand caresses my cheek.*

I hold my gaze on the sheet, barely blinking, and will more memories to come. But it's no use. That's it, that's all, folks. A headache builds in my temples. I turn onto my back, lower the blankets and glare at the ceiling tiles.

Why did this happen? Why did a supposedly domesticated bison bull decide, on one spring day like any other, to go after me in a two-thousand-pound rage? Am I such a total loser that God or the universe or whoever decides such things considered my life so useless it should be erased in one fell swoop?

Panic—or maybe terror—grips me so suddenly that I sit up, clutching at the sheets. I bite my tongue hard to keep myself from screaming, but I can't fight the energy surging through my arms and legs. I punch at the bed, rip the sheets, kick the bedside table. A mug the Woman must have left after her afternoon tea smashes to the floor. My body is shaking, and the feeling isn't gone yet, so I spring out of bed and stomp on the pieces of mug. I feel pain through my fuzzy socks, but the crunching sound is soothing somehow. I jump harder. A shard of porcelain jabs into my heel, and I yelp but can't seem to stop. I am about to pounce again when I hear a voice at the doorway.

"Jessica." I ignore the voice, leap anyway, but it interrupts my fun again. "Jessica!"

I swing around and see a nurse standing there, a tiny lady with a tight ponytail. Her hands are firmly on her hips, and I laugh the loud and obnoxious guffaw of a madwoman. *And just how are you going to stop me?* I'm thinking, but then through the door steps another nurse, about a foot taller and a hundred pounds heavier than the first. They move toward me in unison, and I let out a scream that sounds like it comes from an animal.

I can't remember, and I can't love. But I am very good at getting pissed off.

# Step by Step

Put one foot in front of the other.

Sounds easy enough. To a fully functional human being, that is. I observe my bare feet, the flakes of metallic-blue polish remaining on my nails (pre-coma, because I don't remember painting them), and will them to move carefully and deliberately. They're tender where I stomped on the broken mug, but that's a minor irritant compared to the challenge of getting my feet to follow my commands. Sure, I can walk to the bathroom and down the hall, but I am not as precise and quick as I should be, and they are making me practice with Ruby, the rehab lady.

Ruby must have read a lot of books on how to encourage the brain-damaged, because she never stops saying nice things, no matter how much I suck. "Good job!" "Keep trying!" "You're almost there!" "You rock."

I bet I'd get an Olympic medal if I could actually walk in a line that even resembled straight, instead of this invisible zigzag trail I follow through the rehab room.

"Don't worry," Ruby says. "Your brain and legs need to relearn how to communicate with each other, but it's going amazingly well. You'll be running circles around me in no time."

So we try again. And again and again. I stand at attention, try to buy into her praise and follow her lead. We stand on one foot, we touch our toes, we touch our noses, and we play Head, Shoulders, Knees and Toes. Next it's Simon Says.

"When will I be ready for dodgeball?" I ask. Her face falls, and she struggles to find a way to let me down gently until she sees my smirk. She cracks up.

"You're a nut," she says, throwing one of my balled-up socks at me.

"Well, at least they didn't have to tie me to the bed today," I say.

I don't get a laugh with that one.

Back in my room, I stand and study the parking lot outside my window. It's windy, and swirls of dust dance around the cars. When I turn around, Super Doc is leaning against the doorframe.

"Rough day yesterday, I hear," he says.

My throat tightens. What did the nurses tell him? Psychotic episode, or maybe severe mental breakdown involving mutilated bedsheets and a smashed piece of china?

"Got a little frustrated," I say.

He walks across the room and settles into the chair. "Did the medication help?"

"Uh-huh. Knocked me right out."

He nods. "Anger issues are pretty common after brain trauma," he says. "You're facing a lot of challenges, plus chemical changes in your brain can affect internal impulse control. I'll be sending someone over to help you with that. Her name is Dr. Kirschbaum."

I nod. I can't imagine what she can do to get me to chill out, but there is no saying no to Super Doc. It would feel like saying no to God.

"Until then," he says, "have you tried counting to ten?"

Counting? That's something you'd say to a preschooler having a tantrum over candy. I shake my head.

"It sounds too simple, but it helps. Gives your body a bit of time to come down from the adrenaline rush. Take deep breaths too. Works for me." It's hard to picture Super Doc ever coming undone, but I'll take his word for it.

When he stands up, he puts his hand on my arm. "Other than that, how are you feeling? How are the headaches?"

"Not so bad," I say. "I can take it."

"Good attitude. See you soon then." On his way out, he stops and looks at the bulletin board again. "Any of this seem familiar?"

All I can do is shrug. I don't want to give an answer that is too pessimistic, or he might give up on me. "Now that I've been staring at them for days, I can't tell."

He nods. "Give it time, Jessica," he says. "These things don't happen overnight."

# Trivial

Late afternoon. The Parents have not yet arrived, and the walls of my room are closing in on me. My head aches, partly because of the whack to my skull but also because of boredom. The only things in the room with any color, any evidence of the real world, are the photos on the bulletin board. Looking at them, though, only makes my temples throb more.

I place my hand on the phone and think about calling someone. But who, and what would I say? *Hi, remember me? I don't.*

I need to get out. I take careful steps through the doorway and glance down the hall. The coast is clear. There's a TV lounge at the end of the wing that's always empty when I walk by on the way to rehab, so I shuffle my way over to it, one foot in front of another. Mighty fine walking for a little brain-dead girl.

But when I step into the lounge, a crowd is sitting on the couch. I freeze in the doorway. A girl with dark-purple hair and two nose rings looks up at me, then nods hello before turning back to the TV. I wonder how crazy it would look if I hightailed it back to my room. Nose Ring girl glances at me again; I must look like a deer caught in the headlights, because she gestures to the empty armchair in the corner.

I sit down quickly and turn toward the TV. Ridiculous, I know, but my heart is pounding. Not only did I lose my past, but it seems I lost all my social skills too.

*Jeopardy!* is on, and a lanky boy with a neck brace sitting next to Nose Ring girl mutters, "Alvin" in response to the square that says, *Theodore, Simon & he formed the famous musical trio.* The contestant says the same. Alex Trebek declares, "Yes, that's correct for $200!" and the neck-brace guy high-fives a chubby boy next to him. Nose Ring girl rolls her eyes at me.

"Doorknob over here thinks he's a genius," she says. Brace guy flips her the finger before turning back to the TV. And on it goes. Brace guy answers questions, and sometimes he's right. Chubby boy cheers him on; Nose Ring girl makes sarcastic comments. When the show is over, they all stand up and stretch.

"Well, that was a slice," Nose Ring girl says to me. Then they are gone, and I am alone in the lounge, watching a woman squirt stain remover on her son's soccer clothes. From her smile, it looks like it's the most exciting part of her day. And sadly, being in this lounge was the best part of mine.

# She Calls

It's 3:37 AM. The blanket feels stiff and scratchy against my cheek, and my stomach growls. I click on the lamp and swing my legs over the edge of the bed. I wonder what Jessica did when she couldn't sleep in the middle of the night.

I don't have to go to the bathroom, but my feet make their way across the room. Once inside, I click on the light. There she is, waiting for me. The Girl in the Mirror.

"Me," I whisper. Her lips move in unison with mine.

Though she is a stranger, she is becoming a familiar one. Like someone you see every day in passing, on the bus or walking their dog in the neighborhood. The details of her face are no longer new and interesting. Now that I have studied every line and curve and freckle over and over, I have progressed to taking in the whole of her—the way she looks back at me, the first impression she must give. Is she pretty? I decide that, yes, she is. She may not exactly turn heads, but she has a pleasant-enough face.

I imagine that I am meeting a boy for the first time and stretch my mouth into a smile.

"Hello," I whisper, "my name is Jessica. But you can call me Jessie." Surprisingly, my cheeks flush to a soft pink. Jessie must be a shy person.

I stand there a few more minutes, staring at the reflection in front of me. My feet are cold on the tile floor, and finally I click the light off and make my way back to the bed. I pull the blankets over my head and listen to my breathing. She is shy, I repeat in my head. I am shy. I close my eyes and a shiver goes through me, but I'm not cold.

I have to get to know her again. "Goodnight, Girl," I whisper.

# It's All F
## Game
### Someone
#### Loses an I

I've just woken up from my second siesta of the day when the curtain swishes open. A woman with long black hair and café-au-lait skin steps up to my bed.

"My name is Dr. Kirschbaum, but everyone calls me Dr. K.," she says. "I'm a neuropsychologist." She shakes my hand, then fans her face with her hand. "I can't believe how hot it is, for spring. An absolute furnace. My makeup must have melted all over my face."

She looks perfect, like she's stepped out of a fashion magazine. So this is the miracle worker Super Doc has sent to help me with my temper. "I'm here to ask you a few questions. Do you feel up to that this afternoon?"

"I had plans to go bungee-jumping," I say, "but I suppose I could cancel."

Her laugh doesn't suit her at all—it's loud, a little obnoxious. I like her more already. "You seem to have

wits about you anyway." She pulls a notebook
and a deck of cards from her bag. "So, we're going to
do a sort of test. First I'll show you cards with faces.
I want you to tell me the names of the people. Then I'll
ask you questions. Just answer them to the best of your
ability. And a tip: it's better to guess than to say you
don't know."

She sits down. The first card is so easy I roll my eyes.

"Michael Jackson," I say.

"Is he alive or dead?" she asks, and my reply—"He
beat it"—gets a grin.

The next is equally challenging.

"President Obama."

And so on and so on. She shows me famous actors
and singers and a few politicians, and I know them all.
I don't have to guess. She smiles encouragingly after each
answer, and I start to feel like an idiot. *Big deal*, I want
to say. *Of course I know these people. I would have to have
lived in a bubble for fifteen years not to.*

When the cards are done, Dr. K. exclaims, "Excellent!"
and scribbles something in the notebook. Probably something like *Recognizes everyone in the whole damn world
except herself.*

She says it's time for part two, and I brace myself for
the worst—what's your favorite color, what kind of food
do you hate, what are your hobbies, blah, blah, blah—
but instead she comes out with, "What is the capital city
of France?"

I'm annoyed—what does any of this have to do with my tendency to freak out?—but I think maybe this is a test to see if I will lose it again, so I play along. I answer, one after another, questions about geography and famous dates. I get a few wrong, I think, because she writes something down. But it doesn't seem to be a big deal. At the end she says, "You've passed with flying colors." Then her face turns serious, and she leans toward me.

"How are things going?"

An uncomfortable feeling creeps though me, and the only thing I can think to call it is embarrassment. I passed, but everyone knows by now that my brain is defective and I can't remember anything that matters.

I shrug. "Should I guess?" I ask.

She nods slowly, as if she understands exactly what I mean. "I can only imagine." She stands up and tucks the cards and notebook back into her bag. "That was great, Jessica. A good start. I'll come back in a few days, if that's okay?"

I nod, and she's almost out the door when I say, "Dr. K.?"

She turns around. "Yes?"

"You look like Pocahontas."

I get a smile.

"Aren't you supposed to help me get a grip?"

Her face turns serious. "I need to do a few assessments to make a plan for our therapy. Then we can begin the real work. See you soon."

I sit on the edge of the bed, the word *therapy* hanging in my mind, and a feeling of loneliness sinks in. I know that Nelson Mandela is dead and Avril Lavigne is alive and kicking. I wonder what I'd say if Dr. K. flashed me my own picture.

# Oscar-Worthy

Another morning with Rehab Ruby, and I kick butt. "Wow," she says. "Your progress is mind-blowing." And I think she means it. Back in my room, I take a shower, then watch the birds flit from tree to tree outside my window. Mother and Father are staying in a small apartment the hospital provided, but they have to take turns going back and forth between here and the ranch to take care of the bison and so Stephen can go to school. They've told me the schedule, but I can't keep track of what day of the week it is and who I'll see when. They have lives; I don't.

But if I want to get my life back, I can't hide out forever waiting for some magic cure. A surge of determination comes over me, and for lack of anywhere better to go, I trudge down the hallway to the TV lounge.

The girl with the nose rings is there again, stretched out on the couch with her feet crossed on the arm.

She's flipping through the channels with the remote, and the flicker of a smile crosses her face when she sees me.

"Hey, hotshot. What's going on?"

My face gets warm, but I hold myself together enough to squeeze out, "Not much" before I plunk down into the armchair. We peer at the TV, and she keeps clicking until she stops on a scene.

"Ooh la la," the girl says. "What happened to Felonia?"

On the screen, a woman lies in a hospital bed, her blond hair spread out across her pillow like a silk fan. A machine connected to her by wires emits high-pitched beeps. One perfect scratch, bright red like her lipstick, angles upward from her eyebrow to her hairline. Her eyes are wide, and despite her condition, she is stunning.

A square-jawed man walks up to her bedside and clutches her hand in his.

"Felonia, my darling, I'm so sorry. It's all my fault. If only I hadn't decided we could drive through that storm, this never would have happened."

Her eyes, though I didn't think it was possible, open wider. "Storm? When?" she says.

The square jaw falls slightly, and the handsome man leans closer. "Don't you remember the accident?"

"Accident?" she says. "What accident?" Her voice rises to meet the beep of her monitor.

The man swallows. He speaks slowly, afraid. "Do you even know who I am?"

"Should I?"

The camera zooms in on his face, the man's mouth hanging open in shock. "I am Sam, your fiancé," he says. "And I think you have…amnesia!"

Violin music plays as the scene fades to black and a deep voice announces, "In tomorrow's episode—"

Nose Ring girl sighs loudly and changes the channel to where Alex Trebek is waiting for an answer. Or rather, a question.

"How lame," she says, turning toward me. "So what brings you to this lovely place?" She gestures to my patch of shaved hair. "Were you in a car accident?"

My mind scrambles for the right answer. I can't exactly tell her that I'm much lamer than any character on a soap, that my story is true. I am a real, live, breathing cliché. I clear my throat.

"Something like that" is all I can say. She scrutinizes me, her brown eyes dark and intense against her purple hair, trying to figure me out. I stand up before she can find out there's nothing to discover. "Bye," I say. And Ruby would be proud to see that I walk in a perfectly straight line down the hallway and back to the cocoon of my room. I hide there for the rest of the day, picking at my lunch, flipping through TV channels and dozing. So much for progress.

After dinner, Mother is there to tuck me in. "Sorry I wasn't here earlier. Stephen had a science fair," she says, placing a stack of magazines on my bedside table. "Grabbed these from your room at home."

She stays for a bit, filling me in on Stephen's magnetism project, until my eyes get heavy. She stands up and gives me a quick peck on the forehead.

"I love you, Jessica."

I feel flushed suddenly, like someone has blasted a blow-dryer in my face. I swallow, uncertain what to say. But before I have time to think about it, she is out the door. It clicks shut behind her.

It's not the first time she's said *I love you*, but it's the first time I've felt a reaction when she did. That warmth could have been a genuine response to what another human being has said. Or maybe it was only nervousness, a fear of saying or doing the wrong thing.

Or could it be, maybe, that I am beginning to care?

# Never-Never Land

S tephen and I stand in front of the elevator.

"How long do you think they'll be?" he asks.

"Awhile," I answer. "Those doctors are always running behind."

My parents are meeting Dr. K. today, and I wasn't invited. But that's okay, because I get to have some time alone with Stephen, away from Mother's protective gaze. She even said we could go for a walk in the hospital if we stick together, and Stephen assured her that he would oversee my whereabouts. I get the feeling, from the words he uses, that he isn't your typical ten-year-old boy.

"Where are we going?" I ask.

"Where do you want to go?" he asks.

I picture the two of us sitting in the cafeteria, with its weird smells, sharing a dry muffin that's been here longer than I have. An idea forms in my mind. "How about we play pretend? Like that caravan game or something?"

His eyebrows rise in surprise. "Here? I'm not sure this is the place—"

I clasp my hands tightly in front of me, begging. "Pretty please? It'll be like old times."

A strange expression clouds his face, and he's about to speak when the elevator dings and the doors slide open. We step inside, and the doors shut. Stephen glances at me, then points his finger and slowly, purposefully, pushes the B button.

"All right," he says. "Let's explore then."

"That's my boy," I say. But, strangely, now that he's agreed I feel jittery. Since waking up from the Big Sleep, I've gone up a few floors in the hospital for tests, Mother holding my hand, and made a few trips to the cafeteria. Otherwise, the Head Trauma Unit of the hospital has been my whole world.

The elevator lurches to a stop, and the light above the door reads *B*. The doors slide open to reveal a concrete wall.

"Thumbs-up or thumbs-down?" Stephen asks.

The wall isn't exactly calling to me, but the last thing I want is to go back to my room. So I give a hesitant thumbs-up. He leads me by the hand into a cold, damp tunnel. "It's fantastically sinister down here," he says.

He's right. The place gives me the willies. There is no sound, no life. But I force myself to move, to fall into step beside Stephen. This is what I asked for. Little Man rolls his eyes and twists his mouth into a ghoulish expression.

"Isn't it faaa-bulous being a vaaa-mpire?" he says in a deep voice, rubbing his hands together. "I think ve vill find some veddy scrumptious prey in this place, no?"

I nod. "Yes, yes, I think so." I'm surprised how easily and naturally he throws himself into the game. He must have been missing this, been waiting to have some fun with the Girl all this time.

"Zen ve must walk like zis," he says, hunching low and narrowing his eyes. He creeps down the corridor. I stand and watch him until he skulks back toward me. He puts his hands on my shoulders. "Vat is ze matter? Have you forgotten everyzing I have taught you?"

I hunch down too and try to make the same diabolical expression. But I have a feeling I look like I'm constipated. "No, no, of course I haven't. Vere are ve going, master?"

"To ze catacombs," he says. "Zere vill surely be some poor lost souls vandering zere, just for us."

"Faaa-bulous," I say. And together we lurk down the tunnel. It takes a few minutes, but I start to forget that we are in a hospital and don't think about the fact that I am too old to be playing such games. We explore the basement as hunters of the night. I am no longer Jessica the girl with brain damage. I am a vampire, on the prowl for blood.

We reach another elevator, and Stephen stands straight. "Ve are going back into the world now," he says, pushing the call button, "and ve must hide our real identities. You call me Stephen, and pretend I am your brother."

I am a little sad to end the game, but of course it cannot go on forever. I stand straight too, and then the elevator bell dings. A man in scrubs nods at us as we step through the doors. "Which floor?" he asks.

Stephen looks at me with a raised eyebrow.

"Um," I say, "twelve, please." The top floor, not back to the Head Trauma Unit. Stephen winks at me.

I'm starting to get into the swing of things.

---

When nine o'clock comes and it's lights out in the ward, I lie on my back, gaze up at the ceiling and replay the afternoon with my brother. It all seemed real, like a spell had been cast over us and turned us temporarily into real vampires. Pretending we were time travelers from the future in the Cardiology department on the twelfth floor was magical too, until I started to crash and Stephen had to lead me by the hand back to my room. I could barely keep my eyes open during dinner with the family at the cafeteria, and they left early to let me rest.

The time I shared with Little Man was weird and crazy and made me forget all the things that are wrong with me. I'm not clear on how this memory thing works, but I think I will always remember today.

# Rotten Luck

Day fifteen post-coma. My fun with Stephen has me feeling gutsy, alive. Out, I tell myself. I need to get out of my room.

Nose Ring girl is in the lounge when I arrive. The TV is off, and she is flipping through a magazine. She sees me glancing around the room in search of the remote.

"Lost," she says. "Maybe one of the guys hid it. Ha-ha, so clever."

I walk over to the TV and click it on, then settle into the ratty old couch. She laughs. "Duh. Why didn't I think of that?"

A little boy is running through a field on the screen, chasing a dog. Happy music plays, and the message *Cheese—Help Them Grow* appears.

"How touching," Nose Ring girl says. She throws her magazine onto the coffee table. "Ah, what the fudge. Let's see what's happening to the rich and beautiful today."

The music for the soap, called *Through the Hourglass*, begins. Each of the actresses tosses her hair around as music and the opening credits play. I grit my teeth. I could get up and change the channel, or I could leave without knowing what happened to Felonia and her amnesia. But part of me wants to know, needs to see what happens to her. Did they strap her down to the bed?

After a recap of last week's events, the action picks up at the hospital. A doctor—a Leonardo DiCaprio look-alike—stands over Felonia, a clipboard in his hand. "I'm sorry I have to be the one to deliver the bad news," he begins in his manly voice, "but the tests have verified what we feared was true. In the accident, part of your cerebellum was damaged. And unfortunately, it is the part that controls your memories."

Felonia gasps and clutches her perfectly manicured hand to her chest.

Idiotic soap. They can't even get the anatomy right: I know from Super Doc that the cerebellum does not control memory. The frontal and temporal lobes do.

Dr. DiCaprio puts the clipboard down and sits on the edge of the bed. He takes her hand in his. "I can only imagine how difficult this must be to hear. If you need anything, anything at all, I will be here. Day or night."

The scene fades to black as the two of them gaze longingly into each other's eyes. The next scene begins at a gravesite with a woman holding a bouquet of flowers, but I am not listening. My heart pounds. There is no cure, I am thinking. Nothing can be done.

"She's lucky," Nose Ring girl says suddenly. She glances at me. "Felonia. She's lucky."

I am afraid to ask, afraid to enter into this conversation. But I have to know what she means. "How's that?"

She sighs. "Think about it. How many people get a chance to start fresh like that?" Her dark eyes glisten in the bad fluorescent lighting.

I could come clean, could tell her that she's looking at one of the rare few lucky enough to get a so-called fresh start. But I didn't come to the TV lounge to expose my secrets.

"I would give anything to have my whole miserable past erased," she continues, propping her feet on the coffee table, "to be given a clean slate." She raises her hand and snaps her fingers. "Poof. Vanished."

She's looking at me, waiting for me to agree. Her idea is a lake in my mind, and I dip and splash through its murky waters, trying to make sense of it. Lucky, she thinks. What comes out of my mouth is not what either of us expects. "What have you done that's so bad?"

Her eyes narrow. "Well, we're getting mighty personal, aren't we?"

This means nothing to me, but, of course, she has no idea. You need to have a personality to think something is personal. "I guess so," I say.

She studies me carefully, her hands gripped tightly on her lap. "I don't even know you."

I let out a snort of laughter. "I don't know myself either," I say.

One of her eyebrows rises, but she doesn't ask what I mean. "Oooh. That's deep." The wheels of a cart squeak as it rolls by the door. She glances at the hallway, then stands up. "I should get going before my mom throws a fit."

Once at the door, she turns back toward me. "My name's Tarin. I'm visiting my gran. She had a stroke."

She waits for me to tell her what I'm doing here. I fake interest in the commercial for a kitchen gadget that chops veggies at the speed of light.

She takes the hint. "Stay cool." Then she's gone.

The soap is back on; the woman at the gravesite is on her knees, sobbing. But I'm not absorbing a thing. I'm thinking about what Nose Ring girl—Tarin—said, wondering if she truly meant it. It's hard to believe anyone could be crazy enough to want to have amnesia.

Felonia is lucky, she said. Lucky is discovering a suitcase of money in your attic. I doubt that a two-thousand-pound bison playing a solo game of rugby with your head can ever be a good thing.

# Miss Congeniality

Early afternoon. Mother is in my room, giving me a mini-lecture on her favorite subject, Life Before the Very Bad Day. Today it's about our summers, and how we usually go camping and I am obsessed with roasting the perfect marshmallow and Stephen puffs up when he gets a mosquito bite. I nod and listen, but all I want is to have a long nap or pick my hangnails. She finally gives me a goodbye peck on the cheek and I curl up on the bed, but the door swings back open.

I think maybe she forgot her purse or something. But when I look up, three girls around my age are standing in the doorway. One is short and athletic-looking, with blond hair pulled back in a ponytail. Another looks like a little waif, with long brown hair parted in the middle. The third is super tall, with a couple of bright-blue streaks in her dark hair. They are all smiling in a friendly-but-terrified way that makes me feel like a specimen in a zoo.

"We just saw your mom," the tall one says. "She said this should be an okay time to come say hello."

The other two nod in unison.

"Oh," I say.

"If that's cool with you, of course," the waif says. Written in bright fuchsia across her shirt are the words *Get a Life!*

I shrug. "Sure."

I know who they are. Mother pointed them out in the photos on the bulletin board, and I have an oversized *Get Well* card they all signed and decorated with lots of hearts and smiley faces. One of them wrote: *The Pink Posse is not the same without you!* They are the Friends. They move together as a pack toward the bed, surveying the room. Their names pop into my head: Cybil, Kerry and Megan. But I have no clue which is which.

The tall one is the first to hug me. I let her, my arms hanging at my sides. "Glad you're okay," she whispers gruffly, her arms tight around me. "We thought maybe we had lost you."

The athletic-looking one gives me a quick squeeze. When she steps back, she smiles but can't look me in the eye.

The waif gives me the longest hug of all, her hazel eyes misty. "We wanted to come ages ago," she says, "but we weren't allowed. God, we've been so worried." Her face is pale with a sprinkling of freckles on her nose.

Mother's head pops in the door, and I realize she has been hovering outside, monitoring the situation. "Everything all right, Jessie?"

"Fine," I answer, and she disappears. It's probably a big moment, I think, this casual-seeming reunion. Likely it has been discussed with the doctors, trying to decide the right time and the right way. Another test of sorts. Will Jessie recognize the Pink Posse? Will she break into fits of giggles, reminiscing over food fights and fashion faux pas?

The tall one doesn't beat around the bush. "So," she says, "do you remember me?"

Something about her is familiar, but it's probably only from the pictures. "I don't know," I say.

She takes my hand and squeezes. This girl exudes confidence, making her seem much older than her fifteen or so years. "Well, that's better than no."

"Stupid question," I say, "but what's your name?"

She blushes. I've caught her by surprise. I try to put myself in her place—one of my best friends survives an encounter with a crazed beast and comes out of a coma, only she doesn't recognize me. I suddenly want to make her feel better, to lessen the blow. "Megan, Kerry or Cybil?"

It seems to work, because she smiles. "Cybil."

The sporty-looking one is Kerry, and the waif is Megan. Now that the names are established, they wander about the room, looking at the photos and checking out the view of the parking lot.

"Any hot doctors?" Cybil asks. Kerry giggles.

I shake my head. "Not in this ward anyway."

"And how's the food?" Kerry asks.

Cybil groans. "You and your stomach, Ker. "

"It's not so bad, if you don't mind roadkill," I answer, even though I barely touch the food. I eat mostly cereal, and so far no one has forced me to finish my other meals.

They all laugh a little too loudly. Kerry gives Megan a look I recognize, one I've seen Mother and Father share. An *Oh poor Jessie* look.

"Well," Kerry says in a slightly high, trying-to-sound-casual voice, "you *were* always complaining that your life lacked excitement."

Megan shoots her a stern look. "Ker! Seriously…"

"Geez," I say, "maybe I should have run away with the circus or something. I could have skipped the part where they drilled a hole into my skull and sucked out the fluids with a mini-vacuum."

An awkward silence; then Cybil puts her hand on my arm. "I think our time is up, Jess. We've been severely warned not to overstay our welcome. We"—she glances at the other girls for encouragement—"we miss you."

I wish I could say I miss them too. Deep down inside, I must. I must miss what they meant to me in my other life. They were the ones who understood what I was going through, the ones I could talk to about stuff.

Stuff, I'm guessing, like boys and tests and clothes and the latest gossip. And now? Well, there is no one who can understand.

"Thanks for coming," I say.

They swarm around me, but they must have been warned not to pet the animal, that she might attack, because instead of the group hug I expect, they give me little pats on my back. Then they rush out of the room.

Mother strolls in moments later. "So?" she asks. "How'd it go? You've always been lucky to have such great friends."

I look over at her, with her naïve, hopeful smile. I can't help it—I groan. "Right, I'm one lucky ducky, aren't I? Maybe I should buy a lottery ticket."

I know it's not her fault that the word *lucky* hit a nerve. But I can't stand it anymore, everyone thinking they know how I feel or should feel or what I should appreciate. Her smile falls like I've slapped her in the face. She must be tired of it all too, because she lets out a defeated sigh and picks her purse up off the table. On her way to the door, she touches me gently on the arm. "I'm sorry I threw that at you. " A quick peck on the cheek, and she is gone.

I am left alone in my room to study the walls and think about the Girl—the old Me—and the new Me, and how much of a disappointment this new version must be. I wonder when the Girl is going to teach me how to play nice.

The lounge is empty when I get there, so I settle into the couch. The remote control has made a reappearance and sits on the coffee table, so I pick it up and switch on the TV. On-screen, a little boy takes a spoonful of soup, then whispers to the camera that it's even better than his mom's. It's midafternoon, so I'm guessing Felonia must be coming on soon. My thumb pushes the arrow button past another commercial—this one for a pocket-sized epilator—then a tennis match, until finally she appears.

Stunning as always, she is still lounging in her hospital bed, surrounded by flowers. The scratch on her face has healed, and her hair is pinned up in a style more suitable for a cocktail party than a hospital. When she picks up a framed picture on the bedside table and clutches it to her chest, the camera zooms in on her face.

"Oh, Sam," she says. "I must have loved you once. Our wedding is set for only weeks from now. But that was before the accident. How can I marry you when you are like a stranger to me? But if I don't marry you, will I be walking away from the love of my life?"

Her lower lip trembles, and tears streak down her cheeks.

This dumbass soap has it all wrong. I should write them a letter:

*Dear* Through the Hourglass,

*Your show is crap. Especially the part about Felonia.*
*I know, because I don't remember my past either. But*
*I would never clutch a photo longingly or blubber*
*over a lost love. I wouldn't because I have no feelings.*

*Yours truly,*
*Jessica*

# Abduction

**M**other, Father and Stephen are all in my room first thing in the morning, waiting to escort me to my big CT scan. I had one when I was in the coma, before they put the tube in for the brain drain, but obviously I don't recall it. Father's eyes have that early-morning puffiness, and he smiles at me as he sips coffee. Stephen is affectionately cradling a calculator, the way most kids would a stuffed animal. Mother is all business.

"Did Dr. Lavoie say what you should wear?" she asks me. "I can't remember if it matters."

I shrug. I let her take care of the small stuff. I'm putting all my energy into concentrating on more pressing issues, like willing that weird, lumpy organ in my skull to wow the doctors today.

Mother digs through my drawers and hands me a pair of yoga pants and a hot-pink T-shirt with *Little Miss*

*Sunshine* written across the front. Hands shaking, I slip on the clothes in the bathroom.

The scan is only to check how the healing is progressing, Super Doc said. It's not the Final Word. But I can't help wondering what will become of me if it detects what I fear most: that I am not getting better at all, that I am damaged beyond repair.

Once dressed, I stare down the Girl in the Mirror. "Kick some ass today, okay?" I whisper. She nods, but her eyes are huge, like a scared puppy's.

---

We march down the hall, the four of us, on our mission to the eleventh floor. I am hyperalert: I can feel my heart beating in my chest, my feet touching the floor with every step, Mother's hand on my lower back. I am fully here, in the moment, not the Sleeping Beauty of a few weeks ago. That should count for something, shouldn't it?

A short woman with spiky blond hair is in the scan room when we get there, and after a brief "Hello Jessica, my name is Donna," she launches into a speech describing the test procedure and the rules I have to follow. I have to take off any jewelry. I have to wear the most ridiculous-looking gigantic helmet that must weigh a hundred pounds. Donna excuses herself for a moment, saying she needs to do something on the computer in the other room.

The door closes behind her, and Stephen leans in toward me.

"Be brave, my friend. I know you must be scared," he says, "being the human subject in alien experiments."

Mother shoots him a dirty look. But I laugh, although nervously, and Father chuckles too.

"Please stop them," I say, "if they try to take my brain out through my nostrils."

Another look from Mother, but she doesn't try to put an end to our silliness. There must be a sense of humor somewhere deep down in there.

Stephen is standing up now, his hands firmly planted on his hips. "They are obviously cold, heartless creatures who see us as nothing more than lab rats. We need an escape plan. And we don't have much time!"

I wonder what it's like for him at school. The other kids must either love him or think he's a freak. I stand up too, to join him in the fight. "Yes! How about I get in the scanner, let them think we are cooperating? Then, as soon as they let me out, we hit them with a surprise attack."

He nods. "Unless, of course, I smell burning flesh during the scan, in which case I go after them like a rabid pit bull!"

I laugh, but Father's eyes shoot to the door, and when I turn around, the technician is standing there. Her eyes are narrowed, and I can't tell if she's amused or disturbed.

"The scanner doesn't usually burn flesh," she says, "but we'll keep an eye on it."

Usually? I see then that she's playing along, and my laugh comes out an obnoxious snort. Mother and Father laugh too, and the tech picks up the helmet and moves toward me. At that moment, all the fun Stephen had put into the room vanishes. My body tenses.

Donna raises her eyebrows apologetically at my parents. "Unfortunately," she says, "no one is allowed to stay in the room with you." Mother nods, her face creased with worry, and gives me a tight hug. Father hugs me too, and Stephen gives me a thumbs-up.

I wave to them as they leave the room, like an astronaut about to embark on a shuttle. I want to give them what they want: their daughter and sister back.

"Hook me up," I say.

And so it begins. Donna has me lie down on the bed in front of the scanner, my head fitting into the bottom half of the giant helmet. She gives me earplugs and foam pads to place around my head. She hands me what looks like a video-game controller and shows me the big red button, explaining I can push it at any time if I panic or feel ill or whatever. There will be very loud noises, and clicking and whirring, so she will put some music on for me. I must be careful not to move my head at all, or the photos of my brain will blur. I listen and nod, but inside I am screaming, *Don't make me, please! I'm getting better, I promise! I haven't hit anyone in weeks!*

When Donna finally fires up the machine, the bed I am lying on moves me headfirst into the tunnel of the scanner.

It feels like it's happening in slow motion. The tunnel is not as dark as I expected, and music materializes in my earphones. It's the kind of fluffy stuff most girls my age must like. I examine the beige plastic above me, trying hard to think positive. *C'mon, brain. Show them your stuff.* Even over the music, I can hear the whirs and clicks and shrill beeps Donna warned me about. I close my eyes and focus on the beat of the music, letting it carry me away from this place.

Song after song, more groans and whistles from the scanner, and then the music stops and Donna's voice cuts in. "We're all done, Jessica. The bed is going to slowly move forward so we can get you out of there."

The platform vibrates slightly as it moves, giving me a soft massage, and the light grows bright. I think about death and the light at the end of the tunnel. I don't know what's wrong with me, but when I emerge my eyes are watering, and I'm not sure if it's from the machine or... could I actually be crying? I reach my arm up to dab at my eye, to see if it's wet, but the door pops open and Mother comes in and grabs my hand midair, clutching it tightly in her strong grasp. She holds it like that until Donna appears and says, "Perfect! You did perfect!" and lifts the monstrous helmet from my head.

# Strangers in the Night

Lights out in the hospital. I lie on my side, mesmerized by the slit of light under my door, and listen to the sounds in the hallway—something beeping, someone yelling. My breathing is deep and slow, and thoughts float in and out of my mind. And though I try not to let the bad ones reach the surface, they are stronger than I am. *I am nothing, I am nothing, I am nobody.*

I squeeze my eyes shut. Jessica the Sweet Thing wouldn't have let such dark ideas take over. She would have fought them off with thoughts of rainbows and unicorns. "I can be her," I whisper into the darkness. But it sounds empty and meaningless. A lie.

Sitting up, I click on the bedside lamp, grab a magazine and flip through the pages. Aqua eye shadow is hot, but pink is not. Ankle bracelets are in again, wrist bangles are out. Working out is cool, but BO is nasty. I am at the last page and ready to declare myself a fashion expert when a small piece of paper flutters out and disappears under the bed. Down on my knees, I reach past the blanket hanging over the side and grasp about until my fingers hit pay dirt.

*Jess, you old cow. Happy Birthday!* the note says in orange ink. A big heart with *Love Ya Forever* is on the other side, and it's signed *Best Friends Always, Megan.*

My fingers trace the shape of the heart carefully. Only a few short weeks ago, before this shitty thing happened and I was turning fifteen, I was somebody. All that I had before has to be up here in my head somewhere, lingering, hiding in the shadows. My hand is shaking as I put the note down on the table, and a number appears clearly in my mind: 770-2865. And I know. That is Megan's number, one I probably used to call several times a day.

She was there for me. And she would be now, wouldn't she? She seemed to care when she visited with the Pink Posse. If we were as close as it seems we were, this whole thing must be tearing her up.

I pull myself up on the bed and stare at the phone. It's late, and Megan might be sleeping. But I probably called her late at night all the time before, to talk about homework and guys and whether I should wear aqua or pink eye shadow. Wouldn't she be happy to hear my voice? Wouldn't it feel like old times?

I pick up the receiver and dial slowly, my heart beating hard in my chest. I am not a nobody. I have a Best Friend Always. The phone rings once, twice, and I am thinking about hanging up when there is a click and a soft, sleepy "Yes?"

Nothing comes out of my tight throat, but my breathing is so loud she must be able to hear me. Does she know it's me? Would the hospital's number show on caller ID? I clamp my hand over the receiver, panic taking over. What was I thinking? She used to be my best friend, but that was a whole other life. That was then; this is now. And now is very, very different.

"Hello?" Her voice is louder now, more awake. "Anyone there?"

The loneliness that has been creeping through my system all day makes me want to cry out and say, *It's me, your friend, and I miss you, or at least I think I could, and do you think about me? Maybe we could talk—like, really talk—about the way things were before and things that matter and the way things might be again if I can beat this stupid thing.* But instead, with shaking hands, I place the receiver gently back in its cradle. I curl up tightly in a ball on the bed and wrap my arms around my legs.

What color eye shadow to wear isn't exactly a life-or-death decision. But what about the other stuff? There's no one I can talk to, no one who will genuinely understand what it's like to lose everything. It's not advice on makeup that I need. It's someone to tell me that everything is going to be all right.

# System
# Malfunction

I'm back from another march around the rehab room and contemplating a shower when Mother and Father and Little Man show up. I know right away that something is different. There's a stiffness in the way they walk. After polite hellos, Father announces that Dr. Lavoie wants to talk to them about the results of the CT scan.

"I'm coming too," I say. Mother and Father share a look that says, *Oh no—is this going to set her off?*

I soften my voice, trying to show them I can be reasonable. "Please," I say, putting my head on Father's shoulder. "I promise to be good."

Mother sighs. "I'll go ask." When she's gone, I go into the bathroom and have a brief staring contest with the Girl in the Mirror. I win. There's a knock on the door, and Mother tells me from the other side that Dr. Lavoie has said it's all right, but Stephen has to stay in my room.

I open the door and blow Mother a kiss. "You rock,"
I say, and she blushes.

———

Super Doc's office is perfectly organized. The files on his
cherrywood desk are stacked up neatly in the corner.

"Thank you for coming," he says, like he's hosting a
dinner party. "Make yourself comfortable." Mother, Father
and I sit stiffly on the orange chairs and look at him.

"I've got some good news," he says. Mother reaches over
and grips Father's hand. She reaches for my hand too, but
I pretend not to notice and keep my fingers intertwined.

Super Doc smiles that relaxed grin of his, and we all
take a breath. "I'll get right to the point," he continues.
"Jessica, I've carefully studied your file and I think you are
ready to go home."

Mother lets out a little gasp—of happiness, I think—
and Father nods slowly. "Wow. That's great, just fabulous,"
he says.

"I thought you'd be happy," Super Doc says. "It's a
big step for sure. Jessica's rehabilitation has gone so well,
I don't think staying here is in her best interest anymore.
She's healing up nicely, and her motor skills are nearly back
to normal." He leans forward and nods in my direction.
"Of course, you will continue seeing Dr. Kirschbaum,
to help with the transition."

Mother lets go of Father's hand. "So the CT scan results were good then?"

Super Doc leans back again, running his hands through his hair. And that's when I know. Here comes the bad news. He flips open the file in front of him and glances down. "It was difficult to say earlier, because of all the swelling. But now we know. Unfortunately, the scan showed that there appears to be some residual damage to the medial frontal lobe, and potentially a bilateral hippocampal lesion."

"Didn't you say you were going to get right to the point?" I say.

Mother doesn't even flinch at my rudeness. Her shoulders sag suddenly, like the air has been let out of her.

"Well," Super Doc says, unfazed, "it means that the memory loss you are experiencing is not only a result of emotional trauma. It likely has a physical cause. The brain is a very delicate, complex organ and nearly impossible to predict. The damage may repair itself slowly over time. But we have to consider all the possibilities."

"So I might stay this way forever," I say.

Super Doc looks directly into my eyes. Although he's calm, I see a shimmer of a struggle there. Being a doctor must suck sometimes. "Maybe. To be honest, your situation is extremely unusual. Most patients with a traumatic brain injury have other serious cognitive issues as well, like an inability to speak clearly. The rarity of your situation makes it impossible for me to predict the outcome.

We'll continue to monitor things with tests, and therapy will help with the anger and memory loss. But other than that, as hard as this is to hear, all we can do is wait and see. I'm sorry. I really am."

A slight buzzing begins in my head. I get to go home. But there is something seriously wrong with me, something that won't go away by sheer will and determination. Even Super Doc can't save me this time. I should be angry at God and the universe for cursing me this way, maybe grab a picture frame from the desk and smash it against the wall. But, surprisingly, this news doesn't piss me off. In a strange way, I feel a sort of release.

A physical problem. It's not my fault I can't remember things. I can't just snap out of it by trying a little harder.

Mother sits up tall. "But," she says, "why would you send her home when she's not ready? Why does she remember how to walk and talk and the names of famous people, but she doesn't remember her life? It doesn't make sense!" Her voice grows louder. "She needs your help, isn't that obvious?"

I realize then, looking at this woman, that she has been strong, taking care of her family and her banged-up daughter, struggling to keep all these questions inside. Putting her trust in the experts. And now what Super Doc is saying is not fitting into her plan of how things should turn out. I close my eyes as I listen to him try to explain in his usual patient tone about procedural memory, which is how to do things, and how it's different from declarative memory, which is recalling past events. Everyday things like walking and eating and even the taste of foods, he says, are familiar to me. But the events of my life are not, because they are stored in a different part of my brain.

When I open my eyes again, I can see it in Mother's face: she feels ripped off. My thoughts spin so fast—*going home, physical cause, extremely unusual*—that I can't decide how to feel. The Girl, wherever she's hiding inside my mind, must be celebrating. Home at last! Out of this cold and impersonal place! But, as usual, she's not communicating.

We wrap up the meeting and walk in silence back to my room, where Mother sits in the armchair and gazes out the window. Stephen tells Father and me knock-knock jokes. *Who's there? Orange. Orange who? Orange you going to let me in?* Mother pops up from the chair and mutters something about the washroom as she scurries out the door.

Father fiddles with a strand of my hair. "I'm sorry," he says, his voice husky, "that your mother is acting like this. She's not herself these days. She just—" He clears his throat. "All she wants is for things to go back to normal."

"I understand," I say.

He lets my hair fall and gives me weak smile. Stephen says, "Hey, did you hear the one about the lion and the monkey?"

Stephen goes on telling his jokes, and Father and I give our courtesy laughs.

Mother wants normal. If only I knew what that was.

# Brush Off

Today is the big day. I will walk out of this place, go to the place I belong. I will sleep in a real bed, eat real food and have a real life. This is good news, and the sick feeling in the pit of my stomach will pass. Super Doc says I can go back to school when I feel ready, maybe part-time at first. I try to picture my high school, but the building could be brick or wood or made out of gingerbread for all I know. I can imagine, though, the stares I will get, the uncomfortable silences that will follow me when I can't find my locker.

Mother, Father and Stephen show up before noon. Father must have convinced Mother not to worry, because she looks happier. They offer to help me pack, but I tell them it'll only take a few minutes, and they should go down to the cafeteria for lunch. Really, I want to do it alone.

The clothes are easy. I throw them in a suitcase. Now there are the pictures on the bulletin board. I grab a bag, and the vacation shot, the first one Mother and Father showed me, comes down first. This family no longer exists, I think. Next is a photo of the Pink Posse, laughing on someone's bed among colorful cushions. I'm shoving it deep into the bag when I hear someone behind me.

"Yo, hot mama." Tarin stands, arms crossed, by the doorway. Her hair is in pigtails, making her look like some kind of punk Pippi Longstocking. It's weird seeing her here, in my space.

"Hi." I turn back to the wall and let my eyes wander across the row of remaining photos. Almost every stage of childhood is represented here.

She saunters up beside me. "Wow, your very own wall of shame." She points to the shot of the Girl in the cowboy hat. "Now that's one to burn."

I pull the pin off the photo, grab it and slide it into the bag.

Finger to her bottom lip, Tarin surveys the rest of the pictures, and when she's done she watches me as I pull photo after photo down and put them with the others. When she finally speaks, her voice is higher than usual, like she's trying to sound casual. "I came to find you because I heard that you're ditching this Popsicle stand. And it appears to be true."

I nod. "I'm going home."

"That's great," she says. "Happy day."

I nearly say that she thinks having crummy amnesia is lucky, but then I remember that she doesn't know why

I'm here. Like how I don't know why she wants her past erased.

"I guess," I say. She raises her eyebrows but doesn't ask what I mean.

Only a few pictures remain on the board, and my hands move fast. I had wanted to let each picture sink in and somehow fill me up, give me some substance to face my first day on the outside, in my real home. But now that she is here, the spell is broken, and I simply want the job done. I finish and place the bag on top of my suitcase.

"Well," she says, "it's been a smash. Maybe I'll see you around."

I try to picture seeing her outside this place. She doesn't exactly fit in with my vision of getting back to "normal." I concentrate on zipping up the suitcase. Nervousness is building inside me, and I feel like making eye contact with her will only make this day harder somehow. That I might fall apart. "Yeah," I say. I glance up, and the usual sharpness in her face has been replaced by something softer.

She moves slowly toward the door, and I know I should say something friendly, maybe give her a high five or something. But I only stand there, stiff and awkward. "Take it easy," she says.

"You too." A final zip and the suitcase is closed. I nudge it gently with my foot.

"Good luck," I say, but it's too late. She's slipped out the door. I'm pretty sure she'll be all right though.

She's tough. It's me, Jessica Grenier, who needs luck the most.

My mother steps into the room seconds later. "You know that girl?" Mother asks. "She's our neighbor Mrs. Meyer's granddaughter. Small world."

I shrug. "Met her in the TV lounge."

Mother puts her arm around my shoulder. "Can't believe this day is finally here. Are you ready?"

I don't have much of a choice. But I nod and smile and act as normal as I can.

—————

When Father and Stephen arrive from the cafeteria, Super Doc and Dr. K. and a straggle of nurses follow them into the room. "Surprise!" they shout, and Super Doc hands me a bouquet of flowers.

"For my favorite patient," he says with a wink. "What are we going to do without you around? You've kept us on our toes this past month."

"You'll find someone else to torture," I say, but actually I am touched. They give me high fives and wish me luck, and my parents thank them for everything they've done. Dr. K. says she looks forward to seeing me soon for our first regular session, And then, as quickly as they came into my life, they go back to their jobs.

With the bulletin board down and all my cards and magazines in a box, the room looks empty and sad.

I am on autopilot, laughing at Stephen's story about talking worms even though I'm distracted. How will I make it out there in the real world? I want to throw myself at my parents' feet and beg, *Please, give me more time here; I'm not healed.* But I can't bring myself to burst their bubble.

"Okeydokey," Father says, suitcase handle in his grip. "Time to hit the road?"

I nod, but my feet don't want to move. "Can I go pee first?"

They laugh, though I don't get why it's funny, so I bolt into the bathroom and close the door. I don't need to pee at all, but I need to see Her. She looks back at me from the mirror with a somber expression. I lean closer.

"I'm crapping my pants," I whisper. Her eyes are cold and hard. No compassion there. "That means I'm scared, dorkface."

The corners of her lips curl up in the flash of a grin, but then she is serious again. "Are you as freaked out as I am? Or are you happy to be going home?"

Her eyes soften, and I see then what the hardness was: a disguise. She's trying to be tough, trying to hide her fear.

"Hey," I say, "you're coming with me, right, Girl? I can't do this alone."

We eye each other, she and I, and my mind races: she had something I no longer have, a connection to the life she had built, a feeling that she belonged. And now she is trapped on the other side of that life, watching me try to recapture what used to be. It must be frustrating, watching some wannabe try to fill your shoes. She probably wishes she could reach across that glass and give me a good smack in the head. The longer I look at her, the more her glare looks like one of disgust.

A sudden knock on the door makes the Girl flinch.

"Jessie? You all right in there?"

"I'm fine," I croak. Now the Girl's eyes are narrowed, her forehead creased. She's got to be worried, like me, and maybe I need to cut her some slack.

"Let's do this," I say. And I open the door to the beginning of the rest of my life.

# Part II

## HOMECOMING

*The pages are still blank, but there is a miraculous feeling of the words being there, written in invisible ink and clamoring to become visible.*

—Vladimir Nabokov
"The Art of Literature and Commonsense"

# The Next Contestant

It happens so quickly. Father puts the suitcase in the bed of a silver supercab pickup, then I am in the backseat, watching the brick walls of the hospital grow distant through the back window. It hits me that I'm clueless about "home." It's in the country, I guess, since we have bison, and certainly not around the corner from the hospital. My family has been traveling a long way to see me, obviously. I am an inconvenience.

Father clicks on the radio, and cowboy music plays while we drive what feels like forever down the long stretch of highway. Stephen sits in the back with me, and whenever I glance over at him he makes a goofy face. An image comes to me, clear as day. *A little boy—Stephen?—his face painted with a fire-breathing dragon that stretches from one ear to the other, the red and orange flames shooting across one cheek. "You're just jealous," says the boy, and tears suddenly start to trickle down, streaking across the scaly body of the dragon.*

The real boy, the ten-year-old, slaps his knees suddenly. "I can't believe you're finally coming home. It's been so weird without you."

I wish I could reach over and touch his cheek, but I don't want to creep him out. So I survey the scene outside, the hay bales, the fields, the occasional herd of horses or cows. We drive and drive, until we slow down near a green sign that reads *Winding Creek, Full Services*. A water tower pokes out of the trees, and a wooden board with the words *Rosie's Café* hangs on the side of a rusted piece of farm machinery by the road. That's all I catch, and then it's empty fields once again.

"Was that our town?" I ask.

Stephen nods. "You blink, you miss it."

We really are country bumpkins. Father turns on his signal light, and we turn off the highway and onto a gravel road. We go over a hill, rocks making dinging noises against the underside of the truck, and when we start down the incline, the other side is a mess of ruts and puddles that look large enough to swallow us up.

"The joys of spring," Father announces. The truck fishtails, and water splatters the windows as he navigates through the puddles for a few miles. Then it slows down, and we turn into a driveway edged by towering pines.

"Home sweet home," Mother says.

We bump down the driveway, the trees on either side swaying slightly under the pale blue sky. We reach the end, where the trees open up to a circular drive. I want a memory to come to me, a glimpse of some happy moment like a water-balloon fight on the lawn or anything fun and light, to cut through the thick blanket of tension in the air. But my mind is empty.

The house is made of wood, with some stonework on the front and a large deck. It fits well with the surroundings—neither big nor small—and there are a lot of large windows and a matching garage off to the side. The truck lurches to a stop and we sit there, quiet, no one moving.

"Welcome back," Stephen says, breaking the silence. Everyone is unbuckling and opening doors, and Father comes around and opens the back door for me. He offers his hand and I take it as I step out of the truck. Somehow my wobbly legs carry me up the front steps. Stephen waves me into the entranceway.

Frames filled with photo collages hang on both walls: a baby girl that must be me, a baby in blue who must be Stephen. Chubby toddlers on tricycles and in blow-up pools, both of us with dogs and kittens—all kinds of cuteness. Stephen pulls my arm. "Want to see your room?"

Mother is taking off her coat, her face flushed. "Don't rush her, Stephen. Take your time, Jessica."

I gaze up at the staircase a few seconds, then take a hesitant step. Closing my eyes, I let my feet try to remember the spacing of the stairs. They stay firmly shut as I ascend, my hand running up the smoothness of the railing. I listen to my body, read the signals that tell me when I have arrived at the top. When my eyes open, I am on the landing. My grip tightens on the railing.

This is it. Our home. My home. Where I grew up. It seems like a nice, cozy place. The kind of place where teenagers run down the stairs on the way to school, their mother calling after them not to forget their lunches. A hint of spice lingers in the air—cinnamon maybe— mixed with a lemony cleaning product. Letting go of the railing, I turn to my left.

Three doors, all half closed so I can't see what lies behind them. Nothing hangs on the door fronts; no clues reveal which one was mine. My family stands behind me. Waiting.

I imagine myself on a stage with spotlights, three doors in front of me. The crowd is hushed, and a man in a dark suit says softly into a microphone, "What will it be? Door number one, two or three?"

"So?" Stephen says, but Mother shoots him a dirty look.

"Let me show you around," she says, but I shake my head.

Father clears his throat like he wants to say something, but he doesn't.

I will go with my first instinct. I will allow no thinking about it, no speculating on where the room of a teenage girl would most likely be positioned in relation to bathroom, parents' room, brother's room etc. I step forward, reach for the door of the middle room. It doesn't neces- sarily feel right, but it's too late now. I don't check for the family's reaction when I push the door open and step inside.

The first thing I see, covering the entire wall but for the window, are three shelves. On them sit what must be fifty or so little figurines, in different positions. Another step, and I see what the knickknacks are. Frogs. Porcelain, glass, plastic, all shapes and sizes. Some are cartoonish, wearing clothes and riding bicycles or carrying fishing rods. Others look realistic, painted in muted natural colors.

Mother comes up behind me and puts her arm around my shoulder. She has a funny grin on her face, like she is about to burst out either laughing or crying.

I did it. I found my room. And when I glance around, there's nothing surprising: it's all sweet and innocent. There's a collage of photos covering half of one wall, mostly of the Pink Posse members making funny faces. A poster on the wall shows a monkey in a suit, grinning. His speech bubble reads *I'm going bananas!* The bedspread is a light-green-and-yellow paisley pattern, and the desk in the corner has a stack of books on it. A cell phone in a hot-pink case sits on top.

It could be a set for a movie, something completely designed and contrived to look like the room of a stereotypical, non-rebellious girl in her mid teens. I'm disappointed. Where are the clues to who this Girl was exactly, to what made her tick?

"What's with the frogs?" I ask, and the grin on my mother's face melts away.

"You collect them. You have since you were little."

"You had a real one for a while," Stephen adds. "An African toad. It lived in an aquarium."

I pick up a ceramic frog wearing a baseball cap and blow the dust off. "And what happened to it?"

"It died," Father says.

"How?"

An odd look crosses Father's face, and he glances at Mother. "You and Stephen took it outside and it ran away."

"We found it later in the bison pen," Stephen confesses. "Flat as a pancake."

I'm dying to say it. *Oh, the irony.* But I bite my tongue and put down the frog.

"Mind if I stay in here awhile? Alone?"

Mother nods, then herds Stephen toward the door. "Of course. It's your room."

When the door clicks shut behind them, I pace slowly around the room. I'm looking, but I'm hardly seeing. I sit down on the edge of the bed, close my eyes and let myself fall ever so slowly backward. Breathe, I tell myself. Breathe in the Girl's air, her space, her life. My muscles relax, and I feel my body sinking deeper, deeper into the paisley. If I lie here long enough, I wonder, will her soul slip back into this empty shell I'm walking around in? Maybe something like in movies, when spirits slide right into someone's body, making their heads flip back and their eyes roll upward?

But that doesn't happen. I lie there, numb, and observe the ceiling, letting the feeling of emptiness sink in to every part of me. I stay like that until a knock on the door snaps me out of my trance.

"Dinnertime," Stephen says.

My head is foggy as we gather around the table and nibble at pieces of homemade Hawaiian pizza. The kitchen is homey, with hanging plants in one corner and colorful ceramic bowls lining the tops of the cabinets. We have banana splits for dessert, in celebration of my return, and after we've cleaned up Father suggests a walk outside.

It all feels surreal, like it's happening to someone else, as I step outside with them, my Family, and take it all in. I am watching a squirrel zip from branch to branch in the pine trees when I feel something bump against my leg. I reach down without looking, and my hand meets soft fur. "Hey, old girl. How ya doing? Did you miss me, Ginger?"

I lean down to pet her, a beautiful golden retriever, and my eyes meet Mother's. She's a few feet away, on the steps, and when I see the expression of surprise in her eyes, it hits me: I knew the dog. No one told me her name. I didn't even see her, but I knew she was there.

"Of course Ginger missed you," Mother says, her voice soft. "We all did."

We make our way down the driveway, my parents, little brother, the dog and I. Stephen and Father chat about hummingbirds and putting up the feeders soon, but Mother is quiet.

I can imagine what she's thinking: How is it that our daughter remembers the dog but doesn't remember us?

# Solidarity

When night comes and it's time for bed, there are hugs and goodnights and way more love than at the hospital. I am alone in my room now, and even though I'm tired, my mind doesn't want to rest. The questions I should have asked Super Doc linger in my mind. When will we know if my life has been completely erased? When am I officially a Lost Cause?

But I can't wait forever for things to come back to me. There are clues all around, now that I'm in the Girl's space. It's up to me to dig deeper. I start with her cell phone. The screen lights up with a photo of Megan and me, faces stuck close together, eyes crossed. I click on the speech-bubble icon, and there's a long list of texts. The last one came from Megan at 11:32 PM a little over a month ago—April 25, the day before the Very Bad Day—and says, Nighty nighty. No worries, we'll ace the test.

My hands find their way, without my having to think, until Facebook is open. The profile photo of the Girl is taken from the side, hair covering part of her face. I check out the Girl's wall and find her last post, also on April 25: it's a photo of a bright turquoise-and-yellow flower. A quote is scrawled underneath in old-fashioned cursive: *And the day came when the risk to remain tight in a bud was more painful than the risk it took to blossom. —Anaïs Nin.*

A link under the image says *The HedgeGod @thehedgegod on Twitter*, which leads to an account with an adorable hedgehog floating in the clouds. *The HedgeGod*, it says, *dispenses quills and quips on the eternal questions of the mind and heart.* The quote the HedgeGod has most recently dispensed is *Don't cry because it's over, smile because it happened. —Dr. Seuss.*

The HedgeGod and his crappy words of wisdom annoy me, so I return to Facebook. I scroll further down the wall, skimming over the posts of videos, photos of funny animals, goofy kids and beautiful scenery, and more quotes. I scan faster, until my eyes water and an ache builds in my temples. Then I shut off the phone and toss it back on the desk. So much there, but nothing that tells me more about the Girl than that she was good at clicking the Share button. Super Doc said it would take time, I remind myself. And I need rest. Lights out. I lie flat on my back on the too-soft bed.

Strange sounds drift into the dark room: a creak, a groan, an electric hum. No nurse will peek in the door to say goodnight; I will not hear the phone ring down the hall at the desk. The only light in this room comes not from the hallway, but from the half-moon outside the window. Everything is so new, so strange. I am in the Girl's space now.

My eyes roam over every fuzzy shape I can make out in the moonlit room: the tiny frog figurines, the stuffed chair in the corner, even the lumps in the blanket where my knees are. I throw the covers off and get out of bed.

I pay a visit to the Girl in the Mirror.

"What do you think of this place?" I whisper. She surveys me with glassy eyes, her lips tightly pursed. Maybe she's annoyed at me for snooping in her cell phone. Or angry that I don't love this place like she does, am not embracing what must be for her a place filled with a lifetime of happy moments.

I lean back and we stare at each other, our arms crossed.

"It doesn't seem too bad," I say. "Except for those dumb frogs."

I'm being an ass, and I don't know why. Jealousy maybe? She doesn't react with anger like I think she will. Her eyes glisten with sadness, and her tightly crossed arms relax to her sides. And then she surprises me. She speaks.

"I feel alone." It is so quiet I barely hear it, but a sharp pain rises in my chest, as if someone has clenched my heart in their fist. Alone. I'm here with the people she longs to be with. But I still feel alone, like her. No one is a winner here.

"Well," I say, "at least we have one thing in common."

I think maybe I will get a smile, but, no, it doesn't work. She reaches up and clicks off the light, and there is nothing but darkness around us both.

# Nostalgia

My first morning at home is uneventful. I sleep in until 11:30 AM; Mother offers to warm up some pancakes, but I choose to eat a bowl of Honeycombs. Father is outside, and when he comes in for lunch, Mother announces that Stephen has something to show us all.

But Stephen does not look enthused. "Do I have to?" he says. Mother gives him one of her steely looks, so he sighs. "Fine."

Mother, Father and I settle into the couch while Stephen hooks a laptop to the back of the TV.

"It's a slide show," Mother explains. "About our family. He made it for school."

Father dims the lights, Stephen clicks something on the computer, and the title *Grenier Family* appears across the screen. Classical music drifts out of the speakers.

The first photo is of Mother as a child, her grin revealing two missing front teeth. Mother groans and acts embarrassed. All I can think is Oh, she used to smile. Then comes Father, maybe around Stephen's age, riding a horse. A cowboy hat twice the size of his head slides down over his ears. The classical music fades, and the perky beat of a pop song begins. The screen fills with a shot of Father with a funky beard, kissing Mother on the cheek. She's got long flowing hair and a gaga look on her face.

"Stephen! Where'd you get that one?" Mother squeals, obviously delighted.

"I have my sources," he says.

A few more photos of the parents' dating days, set to "Moves Like Jagger," and we arrive at the wedding pics. Father reaches for Mother's hand. She is pretty in her white lace dress, and he's dashing in a tux, except maybe for the oversized blue bow tie.

Then there's a photo of a white house, Mother and Father sitting on the front steps.

"Where's that?" I say.

"That's where we lived before we moved here," Father says. "In the city."

"The city?" I say. "Seriously?"

He laughs, but Mother has a funny look in her eyes. "Yes," he says, "we lived there until right before Stephen was born. Before we decided to come out here and experience country living at its finest."

"Your father wanted to get back to his roots," Mother says. She's smiling, but there's a hint of something in her voice. Bitterness maybe?

Stephen clicks again, and now a photo of a chubby-cheeked baby fills the screen. A caption on the screen announces: *Watch out, world! Here comes Jessica.* I am propped up between two pillows on a couch, a tuft of hair sticking straight out of the top of my head.

"Awww," Father says. "I remember that one. That was Easter. Your mother made you that dress."

The outfit has fuzzy pink pompoms dangling from the neckline.

"Made with love," Mother says.

Father chuckles. "And a little cursing thrown in for good measure." Mother doesn't take her eyes off the screen, her arms crossed in front of her like she is hugging herself—or the memory. I picture her young like in these photos, long hair hanging in her eyes, sitting at a sewing machine, concentrating on a tiny dress. Maybe I was sleeping in my crib in the next room as she tried to finish it, late at night, in time for Easter dinner. How she wanted her little angel to be perfect in that dress. And how perfect I was in her eyes.

"Okay, okay, move it along now," I say. Stephen clicks to the next shot: me, elephant legs and double chin, taking a bath in the kitchen sink. Then on and on, more of Baby Me. I lose the big cheeks and get longer hair, and then another caption appears: *And the handsome little devil arrives.* And there's Baby Stephen, leaner than Baby Jessica, with big round eyes.

"Chip off the old block," Father says.

Mother has shorter hair in the pictures, but the glow in her face is as bright as when she held her firstborn. "It feels like yesterday," she says.

We speed ahead through Stephen's babyhood, and in almost every shot I am hovering nearby, the protective—or jealous?—big sister. Then there are shots of us playing together. I am pulling him in a wooden sled; we're wearing giant sombreros and playing maracas; we're all standing in front of a tent.

"That's the time the tent blew away," Stephen says. "Remember? We were chasing it around in the middle of the rain?"

"We?" Father shouts, laughing. "You were crying in Mom's arms because you were scared of the thunder! Right, Jess?" He turns to me, a huge grin on his face, and for a fraction of a second I can see in his eyes that he actually expects me to get in on it, to tease Stephen with him. I struggle to think of something light to say, something not to wreck the mood, because even if I don't remember, I like hearing them talk about it. But before I can, the grin slides away and his cheeks redden. "Or maybe that was another time. Yeah, I think that was near Vancouver somewhere."

"Yeah, the trip to Vancouver—" I begin, because there was a photo from that trip on the bulletin board in the hospital, but Stephen pushes his remote and the next picture grabs my attention. Father and I are standing in front of a fence, and a huge bison peers through the barbed wire to our left. The hump on his neck is covered in thick, dark fur, and his horns have curved tips. This, I'm guessing, is the infamous Ramses.

"Whoa," I say. "He's no cuddly toy."

"Stephen!" Mother protests. Stephen is watching me carefully, like he either feels bad about his choice of photo or is checking my reaction. Or both.

"No worries," I say. "It's not as if it's going to give me flashbacks or anything."

Stephen turns his gaze back to the TV and switches to a new photo.

Mother sighs. "Thank you."

On the screen, Father and I are riding a big green tractor. Then there's the young me, bottle-feeding a bison calf. "That's baby Ramses, believe it or not. You loved the farm from the very beginning," Father says. "Like it was in your blood. Not exactly in your mother's though."

He looks over at Mother and winks, but she does not look amused.

Then there are photos of us carving pumpkins and roasting marshmallows and with baskets of chocolate eggs. The last photo to appear on the screen is the one of us on the beach, the very first photo Mother and Father showed me when I woke up from the Big Sleep.

"Happy times," Father says.

Mother stands up suddenly, her cheeks flushed. "Thanks, Stephen," she says softly. "That was beautiful." She touches the top of my head as she goes by on her way up the stairs. I hear her bedroom door close.

Father and I sit there, watching Stephen unhook the cables. And I wonder if Mother is thinking the same thing I am: things might be different if we had never moved out here to the farm.

# Pandora's Box

It's Monday, and Stephen is back at school. I sleep late again, and when Mother takes out the vacuum after my breakfast, I sneak back upstairs to explore my room more thoroughly. I refuse to become a lost cause.

I turn on the Girl's cell phone again and dig deeper, to older texts. They are mostly from Megan, with some from the other Pink Posse girls and, occasionally, from Mother.

Don't forget 2 bring those earrings

Can I get a ride home from Cybil's?

Did u hear about Kaylie & Brendan? They broke up!!!! OMG!

A lot of everyday stuff and lots of things I can't fully decipher. I didn't exactly expect there to be texts detailing the Girl's thoughts on life, love and happiness. But I can't stop the sinking feeling that I'm getting nowhere.

Next I try Facebook, going more slowly through the posts I skimmed earlier: first the quote about the bud, then a video of a dog imitating a siren, then a surreal photo of a blond model in a flowing white dress and a red scarf, lying across the back of a tiger. From a few weeks of posts, I conclude that the Girl liked motivational sayings, funny little kids and animals, and artsy photos. She put occasional posts on her wall, like *Yumalicious, Mom's making cream puffs* and *What's with zombies? Don't they know they're not cool anymore?*

I sigh and click off the phone. I grab one of the photo albums off the shelf above the desk and flip through the pages, but all I get is Mother, Father and Stephen doing ordinary things and pics of friends at school. One page of the album holds shots of the bison being loaded out of a truck into chutes. The next few pages display my birthday party: Kerry, Cybil and Megan wear silly party hats, sticking their tongues out.

In one shot, Megan's face is covered in icing, and I'm holding a smashed cupcake. Our mouths are wide-open in laughter. I don't feel the tiniest flicker of connection to any of these moments, only festering irritation. When I reach the last page, I slam the book down on the desk.

These pointless snapshots give me no sense of who Jessie was, of the way she saw life. It's not the Girl's fault that her photos are so meaningless. But anger is building in my chest, and it needs to go somewhere.

I don't always have to be good, do I?

I kick my closet door, hard. Pain shoots from my foot to my knee, and I bite my finger to keep from yelling.

I must be demented, because despite the throbbing, booting something that way felt strangely satisfying.

"Jessica?" Mother's voice carries from behind the door. "You all right in there?"

I shake my leg to soften the pain. "Fine," I call. "Just whacked my knee."

"I have something for you," she says. The door pops open, and I glance over at the closet. The dent is too small to notice.

A plastic bag dangles from Mother's hand. "I've been debating whether to give you this for weeks. Since you woke up. I think it's time."

She takes a breath and reaches into the bag, pulling out a Nike shoebox. She cradles it close to her, like she doesn't want to let it go, but finally plunks it down on the desk and places her two hands firmly on the cover.

"I found this after the accident," she says, "when you were still in a coma. I was hanging out in here, because I missed you, I guess, and saw it poking out from under the bed."

A few images pop into my head: a homemade bomb, wrapped in green and red wires, ticking away; a sandwich bag full of white powder. But the Girl seemed too goody-two-shoes to be hiding any terrible secrets.

"There are some papers in there, some notebooks too. I want you to know that I didn't read any of it, not one line." She looks straight into my eyes, and her voice softens. "Even though I was tempted, I have to admit.

When you were in the coma and I didn't know if we'd ever get you back." It's the first time Mother's admitted out loud that I nearly died, like maybe now that I'm home and the danger is past, she can say it. And the way she's looking at me, so intensely, the need she has for me, her daughter, pulls at me.

"I don't mind if you did," I say.

She shakes her head. "That wouldn't have been right. And I'm so happy to be able to give it to you now."

She leaves me standing there, eyeing the box. I'm pretty sure the Girl was squeaky clean. The more I dig into her life, though, another worry more plausible than a dark secret is building. What if I discover I don't like this Girl very much? Then what?

I'm nervous, but I grab the box, sit on the bed and, before I can chicken out, slowly lift off the lid. At the top of the box are loose pieces of paper: two ticket stubs for concerts I don't remember going to, two fortune-cookie papers (*Keep your face to the sunshine and you will never see shadows* and *Help! I'm being held prisoner in a Chinese bakery!*) and a note with the words *I am not afraid of tomorrow, for I have seen yesterday and I love today. —William Allen White* printed neatly on it. I read the words again and again, trying to let their meaning sink in, and then I place the papers on the bedside table.

There are a couple of photos, too, of the Girl with Megan and some guys in baseball caps, sitting on some bleachers. The photos go on the table, and then I pull out a green velvet book with a gold clasp. *Diary* is written in gold-embossed script on the front.

Now we're talking. A deep breath, and I open the cover. The first entry is written in the awkward printing of a young kid, probably grade one or two.

*Dear Diary,*
*I got this from Grandma for Chrissmas. I love it.*
*I love my family. Chrissmas is funn.*

*Yers Truly,*
*Jessica*

Well, that was insightful.

There are only three more pages of entries after that, in the same childish handwriting. They're only a few sentences each, about having a nice day at school and helping Father feed the bison and having a picnic with Stephen on the front lawn. I flip through the rest of the diary, hoping to find some later entries, when she was older and, I hope, less sickeningly sweet, but the pages are empty. I toss the diary onto the desk, and it sends the little papers and photos flying off the edge and onto the floor. I ignore them and reach back into the box.

Near the bottom, there are trinkets that I pull out one by one: a beaded First Nations-style bracelet; a smooth stone with a perfect round hole in the center; golden wire twisted to spell Jessica and then formed into a pin; a plastic toy bison; a peacock feather.

These are childhood treasures, things that must have meant something to little Jessica at some point. I wish I could care about them, wish they took me back to happy times, but they are the trinkets of a stranger. At the bottom of the box is one more thing: a floral spiral notebook with *Journal* on the cover.

I reach into the box, intending to open the cover of the notebook. But I can't do it. Not yet. I toss everything back into the box, wedge the lid on and shove it under my bed.

I have had enough disappointment for one day.

# Icing on
# the Cake

Mother says she has good news: Megan is going to stop in for a visit after breakfast, on the way to her orthodontist's appointment. I go about my cereal preparation nonchalantly, as if my BFF dropping by is no biggie. But I feel jittery as I eat my Fruit Loops. Does she know it was me who hung up on her that night in the hospital? What am I going to wear? What will we talk about? Are two people still best friends if one of them no longer remembers the other? At the hospital, Megan seemed sweet and nice. Everything I am not.

The doorbell finally rings at 10:32, and I saunter up to the door as casually as possible. My best friend, my best friend, I repeat to myself as I pull the door open and turn on a great-to-see-you-but-not-such-a-huge-deal smile. Megan, hair pulled up in a ponytail and lips glossy, stands with a red-haired woman holding a plate of cupcakes. Toothpicks stick out of the cupcakes and plastic wrap stretches over them, creating a domed mini world with pink-icing mountains.

"Greetings. Hello," I say. They say hi back, and then we stand and look at each other, smiling back and forth, until Megan clears her throat.

"Jess, this is my Mom," she says.

I nod. "I guessed that."

"So nice to see you, Jessica," her mom says slowly. "Is it all right if we come in?"

I stumble backward a little and wave them in. "Sorry," I mumble. "I'm such an idiot these days."

Once in the entrance, Megan's mother leans close to me, the cupcakes between us. "Not at all, my dear. To us, you are wonderful. We are so happy you are all right." Her eyes are misty, and I'm feeling bad for making her uncomfortable when I see Megan rolling her eyes behind her.

Mother appears, and everyone exchanges pleasantries. Then, more quickly than I had planned for, Megan and I are alone in the living room. Two cupcakes sit exposed, torn from their utopian bubble, on small plates on the coffee table.

"So," Best Friend says, "how are things going, Jess? Are you happy to be home?" I study her, trying to use my rusty people-reading skills to decide whether she truly wants to know or is only making polite chitchat. She blushes. "Stupid question. Sorry."

I shake my head. "No, no, not at all." I pick up a cupcake and plunge my teeth into the pink frosting.

Megan studies her hands as I munch away. I have no clue what she expects from this visit—laughter, some hugs or a meaningful baring of my soul. I read a magazine article in the hospital about making friends that said you should always "be yourself." Not so easy if you don't know who that is.

There are crumbs all over the front of my sweatshirt when I finish, so I stand up and shake them off. "You'd think I was raised in a barn. Oh, wait—I practically was!" My laugh is too loud. "But let's not talk about me." There's one of the Girl's photo albums sitting on the coffee table, so I open the cover and flip the pages. "What was this all about?"

In several photos, Megan, the rest of the Posse and I have our hair pulled back and wear hockey jerseys and sunglasses. Three guys wearing dresses and makeup stand beside us, hands on their hips.

Megan laughs. "That was for health class. Mrs. Fletcher wanted us all to spend a day being the opposite sex, to try to understand them better. Harrison borrowed your lipstick, so you were pretty psyched."

"Harrison?"

Her eyes widen. I've obviously taken her aback, but she hides her surprise well. "Oh, you know, the guy you like."

I give her a blank look, so she points to the tall skinny guy next to me in the photo. Could he be one of the guys with ball caps in the photo that was in the shoebox?

I can't tell if he's cute or not with the bright pink lips and blond wig. I lean in closer, and Megan flips the pages until she stabs her finger down on a photo of a bunch of guys in regular clothes. "Him. You've had a thing for him since, I don't know, kindergarten or something."

He's okay-looking, I guess. Nothing special. It should bother me that I don't even know who he is, but mostly I am focusing on holding myself together with my BFF.

"Tell me," I say, "what's going down with the rest of the Pink Posse?"

She looks at me with a tired expression. *Yes, honey,* I want to say, *this is Me Being Myself. I don't have much to work with.*

"The who?"

My cheeks feel warm. "The Pink Posse. I thought that's what we called ourselves? You know, the gang?"

"Oh, right," she says. "Only Kerry still calls us that. They're fine. Busy with tests right now, and essays. And we're doing a fundraiser at school to build a well in Africa. A bake sale and stuff."

We look at each other, and my mind scrambles to find what would we have said to each other only a few months ago on this very couch. I come up empty.

"And we miss you, of course," she adds.

I reach down and pick up the other cupcake. "Want one? Made 'em myself." I chuckle at my lame joke, and she gives me a courtesy smile.

"No, thanks. I had one at home earlier."

"Aw, come on," I say. "Live it up."

She shakes her head, and when I glance down at the cupcake in my hand, I am inspired suddenly, not by a real memory we share, but close enough: the photo from my album. The one of me mashing a cupcake into her face.

"Hey, Meg," I say. "Thanks for coming today." She looks relieved and is about to say something when my hand reaches over and smashes the cupcake into her nose. She leaps up from the couch like it's on fire.

"What the—?" she says, covering her nose. "Why'd you—?" She wants to say more, I know, but she's holding back. Taking it easy on her damaged, fragile friend.

"Oops," I say. She is not laughing like she was in the snapshot. Chunks of pink icing slide down her cheeks.

I'm sure we're both thinking the same thing: this new Jessica is completely screwed in the head.

# Cerebral

I lie in my bed, playing the cupcake scene over and over in my head until I am completely disgusted with myself. Then I jump up and face off against the Girl in the Mirror. I give her a pep talk à la Ruby in rehab: "You want your life back? Well then, get your butt out of this room and go get it!"

I march down the stairs, on the hunt for photos, home videos, whatever I can dig up. Mother, in a red spandex outfit that is not her style at all, is sitting cross-legged on the living room floor. A thin woman on TV instructs her audience to breathe, and Mother obeys.

"Jessica," she says between breaths, "want to do yoga?" She brings her hands together in front of her chest, and I try to hide the smirk creeping across my face. She isn't exactly what I'd call a Zen person.

"Another time," I say.

"Tomorrow," she says, leaning forward so her head nearly touches the floor, "I'd like to take you shopping. Maybe get some new summer clothes."

"Whatever."

The yoga must be working miracles, because Mother doesn't blink at my lack of enthusiasm. "Great." She gets up on her knees for what the TV lady calls a downward dog. That's my cue to hightail it to the basement.

I browse the dusty bookshelves for photo albums. There are *National Geographic* magazines, an old set of encyclopedias, books on Egypt, but nothing really meaningful for me to study. At the end of the last shelf, something catches my eye: *The Human Body*. The table of contents shows *Chapter Five: The Brain*. In the dim light of the basement, I learn:

The human brain has almost 100 billion neurons, and from 550 trillion to 1,000 trillion (a quadrillion!) synaptic connections with other neurons.

The human brain generates 12 to 25 watts of power when "awake." This is enough to illuminate a lightbulb.

The weight of the human brain is about 3 pounds.

The brain is about 75 percent water.

While an elephant's brain is physically larger than a human's, the human brain is about 2.5 percent of our total body weight and an elephant's is 0.18 percent. Humans were long thought to have the largest brain relative to their body size than any species. This ratio was supposed to explain our intelligence, but that theory is now known to be false. Many animals, such as mice, have similar ratios.

The human brain is the fattest organ in the body; its solid matter is composed of 60 percent fat.

Your brain uses 20 percent of the total oxygen in your body.

The common belief that humans only use 10 percent of their brains is not true. Every part of the brain has a known function.

Harvard maintains a Brain Bank where over 7,000 human brains are stored for research purposes.

When we are born, our brains weigh about 350-400 grams, and we have almost all the brain cells we will ever have. The baby brain is closer to its full adult size than any other organ in the body.

The human brain reaches its full size in adolescence. It shrinks between 14 and 25 percent in the years to come. The male brain tends to shrink faster than the female one.

At any one moment your brain is receiving about 100 million pieces of information that are fed into the nervous system through the ears, eyes, nose, tongue, and touch receptors in the skin.

The brain can survive four to six minutes without oxygen before it starts to die.

The chapter has a full-page diagram of the brain, the pink and gray parts labeled with their scientific names. There's a section on how memory works, plus brief descriptions of terms like *neurology* and *psychology* and *psychiatry*.

"Jessica!" Mother's voice carries down the stairs. "Want to make cinnamon buns?"

I flip through the pages quickly, my hands shaking. There's one thing I want to know about the human brain, the only thing that really matters. But it's nowhere on these pages. I slam the book shut and shove it back on the shelf.

"Jessica? Are you down there?"

"Coming!" I call, but I don't move—not yet. I lean against the wall and close my eyes. There is no answer to my question. No one knows how to fix a broken brain.

———

Halfway through kneading dough for the buns, I fake a headache so I can hide in my room and learn more online about the brain. Google brings up tons of stuff: a complex, color-coded diagram of the brain's anatomy and scientific articles with words like *oligodendrocytes* and *rhomben-cephalon*. One article leads me to a website all about TBI—traumatic brain injury. There are discussion boards where people have posted topics like *Can't stop losing my temper* and *Dizziness?* and *No one understands*. I pore over the posts, and it's amazing to know I am not alone. But not one person mentions completely losing their past.

Next I search for retrograde amnesia. A news article tells the story of a football player who, after a car accident, lost forty-six years of memories but recovered to become a motivational speaker. Other articles talk about people who arrive in hospitals and can't remember their own names, yet are capable of reciting Shakespearean sonnets or know the capitals of every country.

At the bottom of one site, written in red, are the words *Register to join a TBI support group.* I enter my email address and hit *Send.* Seconds later a message arrives asking me to activate my account. I read it over three times, my finger poised over the mouse.

*No guarantees*, Super Doc said.

But activating my account would feel like admitting that this is here to stay, that I will never go back to normal. I close my email without registering.

I am not ready to go there.

# Shop Till You Drop

When Mother sits on the edge of my bed and shakes my shoulder in the morning, I groan and roll over. But she doesn't give up.

"Jessica," she says, "shopping, remember?"

It's still dark and I'm oh so cozy. But this day is a big deal for her, I bet—a regular mother and daughter going out for some retail therapy. It's a two-hour drive to the big city, so I had promised we'd leave early. I will my eyes to open.

"Be down in five," I croak.

She leaves and I crawl out of bed and throw on some clothes. As I come down the stairs, Father's voice carries from the kitchen.

"Let's cancel it," he says, "and do something low-key. Only the four of us."

I step into the kitchen. "Cancel what?"

Father shrugs. "Oh, a little get-together for my birthday. Your mom goes a little crazy about these things and sent out invitations, like, five years ago. The big five-oh is a big deal, apparently." He stands up with his coffee cup and plants a kiss on Mother's cheek. "Have fun tearing up the town today, ladies."

I scarf down a bowl of cereal and then we are in the car, heading down the gravel road as the sun rises over the fields of hay bales. The windshield is slightly foggy, so Mother turns on the heat. With the warm air and the soft tinkle of gravel hitting the underside of the car, I can already feel my head nodding forward in sleep.

Mother tells me which mall we're going to—the smaller one, with easier parking—and which department stores are having sales. There is no way I will be able to keep my eyes open for the long drive. We turn onto the highway, and a few miles of silence later we pull into a gas station. I pop the door open as soon as we roll up to the pumps.

"Want anything to drink?" I ask. Mother shakes her head.

I'm looking for a bottle of juice in the cooler when I spot something better: a Red Bull energy drink. This could be the pick-me-up I need. The tall blond guy at the cash looks about my age, but I don't recognize him. He obviously knows me—everyone in this small town probably does—because he's watching me with interest as I walk up to the counter.

"Want something with even more kick?"

"Huh?" I answer with my usual wit and charm.

"More of a boost?" He slides a small green box of mints across the counter. "Jolt mints. They're caffeine pills."

I nod and pick them up. He rings up the Red Bull, and I pull the cash out of my pocket to wait for the total. "Four bucks," he says.

"And these?" I ask, shaking the box of mints.

He laughs. "Can't get those here. They're on me. It's the only thing that pulls me through this morning shift. Consider it a little gift, Jess." He winks.

I mumble my thanks. I'm about to push the door open when I stop and crack open the Red Bull. I'm not aware of Mother's opinion on these kinds of things, but I'm sure she has one. I pop two mints in my mouth, chug them down with the Red Bull and pocket the box.

"Whoa!" Blondie says. "That should do the trick."

I wave my thanks and get back in the car. The first stretch of the drive, Mother and I make polite conversation about what clothes I need, Stephen's geothermal experiment in the basement, where we should eat lunch. We don't mention the accident or school or the bison or anything else of any significance. I am kind of enjoying myself. So this is mother-daughter bonding. I can do this.

"By the way," I say, "you weren't going to cancel Father's party because of me, were you?"

She glances at me with narrowed eyes. "Hmmm," she says, and I know the answer. Of course. How can you celebrate and act like everything is normal when your daughter is obviously anything but? It stings a little. The last thing I want to be is a drag.

"I think we should have it," I say. I play the pity card. "Honestly, we could all use a little fun. I'm sick of tests and rehab and serious stuff. I need to get a life again."

She chews her bottom lip. "I don't know—"

"What's the worst that could happen? If I get tired, I'll go to my room and rest. Pinky swear." I stick out my bottom lip in a silly pout, and she laughs.

"We'll see," she says. "I'll talk to Dad about it."

I do a little clap of faux excitement.

Then we are out of things to say. The sun is now shining above the fields that stretch out in every direction, and the only sound is the hum of the tires on the pavement. The seat belt is too tight at my shoulder, and my legs somehow don't want to stay still. I fiddle with the box in my coat pocket, slip two more magic mints into my mouth and swallow without even tasting them.

I feel so awake, but the silence is unbearably heavy. Then it occurs to me: maybe I can use this opportunity to get to know my mother better. Maybe I haven't been giving her a chance.

"So," I say, my voice louder than I mean it to be, "how did you and Father meet? Was it love at first sight?"

Mother glances at me, then her eyes go back to the road. "Well, we met at a dance. I was still in high school, if you can believe that."

"So were you hot for him on the spot?"

Even I am surprised at what has come out of my mouth.

"Excuse me?"

I swallow hard. "Sorry. Cute, I mean. Did you think he was cute?"

"Yes, I did. There was something about him, about the way he carried himself. He was confident, but not arrogant. I was thrilled when he asked me to dance."

"Was he a good dancer?"

She lets out this light musical giggle that I've never heard. I remember the long-haired, big-eyed girl I saw in the old photos. "No, not really," she says.

"When did you know you wanted to marry him?" I ask. "Was it right away? Did your parents like him?" I know I should stop and let her answer, but somehow my mouth won't give it up. "Did you have any other, any other… suitors?" An image of Mother sitting out on a front porch, wearing a dress straight out of *Gone With the Wind*, pops into my head, and I let out an obnoxious snort. "I bet they were pounding down the door."

The quiet that greets me tells me I've gone too far. Mother's knuckles are white on the steering wheel.

I take deep breaths and try in vain to calm this crazy buggy feeling that has now taken over my whole body. She finally speaks, her voice soft but crisp. "There were a few, actually. But I only had eyes for your dad."

"Of course," I say. "I never met the others, but he's a keeper." Change the subject, change the subject, I tell myself, and before I have a chance to consider my choices, my mouth has chosen for me. "You hate the farm, don't you? Are you dying to sneak out in the middle of night with the rifle and shoot all those bison, or what?"

The car veers toward the side of the road. Mother makes an odd sound, like clearing her throat and gasping at the same time. I chew on a hangnail. *Stupid, stupid, stupid.* "I mean, they are ugly, right? And kind of smelly?"

I don't mean a word I'm saying, but I have to have to fill the air, can't keep any random thought in my head where it should stay.

Mother's face is bright red, and I'm sure she's ready to toss me out on the side of the highway. But, unlike me, she can't find her voice.

"Oh my god, I have to pee!" I screech. "Pronto!"

Now the car swerves suddenly to the right, and we lurch to a stop. She turns slowly, deliberately, and glares at me. "What's gotten into you?"

"Brain damage, remember?" I shove a few tissues from a box in the backseat into my pocket, open the door and bolt across the ditch. The long grass is wet and slippery, and I barely make it into the shelter of trees before I have to whip down my jeans and crouch among the pine needles. A feeling of relief washes over me as I go, hands shaking as I pull out the tissue. The air in the bush is fresh and cool. One, two, three deep breaths, my pants back up, and I start moving out of the trees.

Odd angles of light land on the car, and Mother gazes out toward the field on the other side of the road, where bales glisten with dew. I see only her shoulder and the back of her head, but I stand there for a minute and watch her. She's a tough woman, and not exactly easygoing. But I want to rush to her, suddenly, and wrap my arms around her and never let her go.

I want to be her little girl again, have her take care of me and tell me everything is going to be all right. But the sad truth is, I am not her daughter at all. I'm a rude, crazy stranger who is posing as her darling Jessica. I move slowly back to the car, open the door and slump into the seat. Energy is still pulsing through my veins, but somehow the spark in me has flickered out.

"Sorry," I say.

She turns to me, eyes red, and nods. We pull back onto the highway, Mother clicks on the radio, and we listen to country music for the rest of the drive.

By the time we make it to the mall, I am less wired. I can act normal—or what is normal for me anyway— and I make an effort to go along with all of Mother's ideas. Yes, jeans, a few T-shirts, a nice top, maybe a skirt. Absolutely, some new shoes and socks and underwear. I follow her around as she plucks clothes from racks and asks me for approval; I nod and occasionally proclaim "cute" or "very nice" for good measure.

We pass through the dress section, and Mother runs her fingers through a rack of floral numbers. "How about one of these?"

I shrug, but she's already checking labels for sizes. I end up trying four in the dressing room, and they all look a little too cheerful on me, with my lopsided hairdo and pale face. But Mother oohs and aahs over a turquoise-and-brown one with satiny straps. I tell her I like it so we can get out of there.

We end the morning with lunch at the food court, and I crash in the car on the way home. When we pull up in the driveway, I am so out of it that Mother has to lead me from the car to my room.

I crawl into bed, clothes and all, and for a few seconds before I drift off, I imagine that I really am her little girl again. Mother has carried me in, asleep, from the car and tucked me into bed. How warm and safe that must have felt, being held in adoring arms all the way to the coziness of my froggy room, knowing I belonged perfectly there with my family, in my home and in the world.

# Poltergeist

I wake up in the middle of the night, my head groggy and my throat dry. It must be the Jolt mints, because no matter how hard I try, I can't get back to sleep. I get up, turn on a light and chug a glass of water.

I was completely whacked with Mother in the car. I've got to get my crap together, at least try to act like a semi-sane human being. And, most of all, I've got to try harder to figure out what made the Girl tick. Down on my hands and knees, I pull the shoebox out from under the bed. I dig the flowered journal from the bottom, take a deep breath and open the cover. There is no date for the entry, only *Dear Me* in a messy scrawl.

*Our new English teacher, Mr. Parent, gave us a weird homework assignment. Everyone complained about it, and so did I—but in the end it got me thinking.*

*We have to write our own eulogy. We can write things we want people to say about us after we are dead. It was harder than I thought. Deep down, I know what people would probably say: that I was a nice person, a girl who followed the rules and always tried her best. But is that all that I am? It depressed me a little to think that there's nothing more memorable about me. Nothing interesting. Here's the best I could come up with.*

There's a folded piece of paper taped onto the page. Finally, something I can sink my teeth into. I open the folded paper and pull my legs up to my chest. I imagine Jessica sitting at the desk, hair pulled up in a ponytail, scribbling away on a sheet of paper.

*On Monday, February 11, Jessica Evelyn Grenier passed away unexpectedly. She was a happy girl, full of life, one who enjoyed nature and the simple things: a quiet walk in the bush, camping with her family, chatting with her friends, taking photographs, a good bowl of cotton-candy ice cream. She grew up on the farm and was a country girl at heart. She loved her dog, Ginger, and the bison she helped take care of on the farm. She left behind her loving parents, Deborah and Ray, and an adoring little brother, Stephen. Though her life was short and she hadn't had time to achieve greatness of any kind, she was happy. And that's what matters.*

A chill goes through me. She couldn't possibly have known that soon afterward she would have a brush with death, and that though she would survive, the girl she had been would cease to exist. Most of all, I'm hit with the unfairness of it all, how she lost that feeling of belonging she once had. Maybe she was boring, but at least she knew where she fit. I read the eulogy again, slowly, until a sound—a creaking floorboard maybe?—startles me, and I look toward the door.

I hold my breath and listen. Another creak, this one louder. Someone is out there. It's probably Stephen or Mother or Father, making a night visit to the bathroom. Willing my feet onto the carpet, I pad softly toward the door. My hand moves toward the doorknob, and when I turn it I suck in my breath. The door is open only a crack, enough for me to peer into the dark hallway. There is no light on in the bathroom, no sign of anyone. The house is silent.

My hand shoots out, pushing the door shut. I toss the journal into the shoebox and shove it into my closet, up high behind a stack of magazines. I scurry back to the bed, bury myself under the covers and pull them over my head. I'm overtired, I know. But I can feel her presence, and it's eerily real. Jessica is here in the house. She's lost and restless, and she wants her life back.

"I won't read the rest," I say. "I promise."

It's probably the caffeine still in my system making me jumpy. But it feels like the Girl is haunting me.

# Human Sacrifice

I avoid Mother the next day, telling her I have a headache and hiding in my room. I find a file called *Home
Videos* on Mother's laptop and watch them one after
another. The clips show the Girl, cheerful and smiling, at
dance recitals and riding horses and playing Frisbee with
Stephen. Physically, she looks like the Girl in the Mirror,
but obviously this brain-damage thing has stripped *that*
girl—me—of any lust for life.

By late afternoon I'm done with all the videos and
starting to feel like a caged animal. When I hear the
rumble of the school bus pulling away, I leap up and practically pounce on Little Man as he saunters up the steps.

"Hey," I say. "Wanna hang?"

He laughs. "Let me have something to eat. Then we
can talk."

I watch him wolf down some cookies. Then he claps
his hands together.

"I've got it! We're going to be anthropologists, and we're doing research on"—he does a drum roll on the table—"African Pygmies! We've been living among them for weeks, learning their customs. And now one of them, a kid we bribed with candy, has confessed that the chief is planning to kill us in an ancient ritual to appease the gods of the jungle."

He looks eagerly at me.

"Cool," I say. I know I am way too old to get into these games, that any self-respecting teenager would have too much pride. But what else do I have going on in my life?

"And then, then"— his eyes widen—"they are going to cook us over a fire and eat us."

The kid is totally twisted. Gotta love him. I raise my hand for a high five, and his face breaks out in a grin.

"All right then, Doctor," he says. "Let's get our gear and head into the jungle. We've got to escape before they tie us up."

I hear footsteps coming up the stairs from the basement, so we race up the stairs and close the door to Stephen's room. "Oh no, the Pygmies!" Stephen whispers, and we both giggle. We throw some essential equipment in a backpack—flashlight, rope, walkie-talkies, granola bars—then sneak back downstairs and out the door.

Stephen glances around the front yard, then peers into the trees. "Well, Dr. Smith," he says in a deep voice, "it appears we have managed to outwit the Pygmies for now.

I don't need to tell you, however, that they are excellent at tracking their prey through the jungle. We must take every precaution, or we will surely end up the main course at their next smorgasbord."

It takes all my willpower to keep a straight face. "Absolutely, Doctor…Doctor…Doctor Pickle." He rolls his eyes but doesn't correct me.

I follow Dr. Pickle as he steals toward the fire pit, glances around to be sure we are safe, then sprints toward the garage. We stand with our backs flat against the wall, our breathing heavy, and listen.

Stephen's eyes are large when he turns to me and grabs me by the shoulder. "We must find our way to the abandoned schoolhouse, the one the missionaries built. The Pygmies are afraid to enter it." He peeks around the corner of the garage, then quickly pulls himself back.

"Who's there?" I whisper.

He leans in closer and mouths, "The chief."

I pull myself flatter against the garage, and we look at each other, holding our breath. "Follow me," he mouths. We move ever so slowly, our backs sliding against the siding, to the back of the garage where it meets the trees.

"On the count of three," he whispers, "make a run for it." He takes a deep breath and starts the count, and on *three* we sprint as fast as our legs can go, crashing into the woods and bounding over rotten logs, until we are so deep into the bush we can barely make out the walls of the garage.

"That was kind of loud," I say, my heart pounding. "Do you think he heard us?"

"Perhaps." We peer through the trees in every direction, and I almost expect to see a short person in a loincloth, carrying a spear, moving through the trees toward us.

Stephen—Dr. Pickle—lets his backpack slide down to the forest floor, opens the zipper and pulls out a notebook. The pages are empty, but he scrutinizes them as though he needs to understand every detail.

"I think we can make it there by tonight." He runs his finger along what I guess is an invisible map. "Are you up for it?"

I nod. "Absolutely." He stuffs the notebook back into the bag and leads our trek out of the woods.

"By the way," I ask, "what happened to the missionaries?"

He shakes his head solemnly. "They got made into shish kebobs."

We walk, squirrels scurrying in the branches above us, until we reach a green shed on the edge of the trees that I hadn't noticed before. "The schoolhouse!" Dr. Pickle says. "Hallelujah."

We bolt quickly to the shed, and Stephen tugs on the door until it pops open. "This should do for the night."

We step inside and are hit with a musty smell like rotten vegetables. There isn't much room between a couple of old lawn mowers and some clay pots, so I perch on top of a mower and Stephen flips over a pot to sit on. We stare at each other, listening for Pygmy chants outside.

The words slip out before I have a chance to think about the repercussions. "Tell me about myself."

Stephen looks startled. "Uh, okay. What do you want to know?"

I want to know everything, every mundane detail of the Girl's life: what kind of movies she liked, what her first word was as a baby, if she was disgusted by fart jokes. At the same time, I am also terrified to learn these details. If I know these things and still catch myself screwing up, it means Jessie is lost forever.

"You know. What made her laugh? Could she be funny, or was she too prissy to let loose? Did people like her? That kind of stuff."

Stephen pushes his glasses up the bridge of his nose. "You mean *you*."

I nod. "Sure, me. Whatever."

I don't think he's going to let it go, but he leans back against the wall and chews on his lip. "Hmmm, where to begin? Do I tell you how much of a royal pain in the butt you were?"

"Ha-ha." I know he's only being Stephen, trying to lighten the mood, but I need this from him. He's the one person I think will shoot straight with me, won't try to soften things or make me out to be an angel.

"Okay, seriously. Let's see. You were sort of funny. You could get hyper and be a total goof with me or your friends. But you were also serious sometimes, like you were thinking about stuff."

"Stuff? What kind of stuff?"

He shrugs. "How would I know? You never told me."

"My bad," I say.

"You liked taking pictures."

I guessed that from all the photo albums in the Girl's room. But I need something, well, less obvious. "Yeah, but what cracked me up? Did I like jokes?"

He scratches his fingernail along the pot he's perched on. "Well, there was a joke about a cowboy you used to tell. Something about falling off his horse into a cow pie. I can't remember exactly. But mostly you laughed at, well, things that happened, not jokes so much. Like when Dad danced around the kitchen with Mom's bra on his head."

Picturing it makes me smile. "This is fun. Tell me everything."

Stephen peers out the streaky window. "Everything?" he says.

"All the juicy details," I say. "Like, was there blood on the ground where Ramses charged me? How mangled was I, exactly?"

He whips his head around to face me. His cheeks are flushed, and something—fear?—flashes in his eyes. "You said we didn't need to talk about it. Remember, at the hospital? You said you were fine now." His voice trembles. I can only imagine what the little guy has gone through, almost losing his big sister and probably getting minimal attention from his parents for so long. It's got to be painful to think about, and now I'm asking him to relive the horror of the day it all began? It's too much to ask.

"You're right," I say. "What does it matter? Look at me, I'm better than ever." I'm mad at myself for being selfish and would do anything to bring us back under the magic spell of our game. "And anyway, I think those Pygmies are hot on our trail!"

I jump up from the lawn mower, grab his arm and pull him up to face those cannibals once and for all.

# Big Shoes
# to Fill

There's nothing in *Seventeen* about what to wear to see your shrink. I grab yoga pants and a hoodie from the back of the closet and pull the half of my hair that's long enough into a ponytail.

It's my first appointment since going home, and there's another drive to the city. No Red Bull or Jolt mints for me this time. I eat a healthier cereal for breakfast, the one with all the raisins, and when Mother, Father and Stephen are at the table, I take the opportunity to make my case for the birthday party. It will be good for me, I say, to be around people again. I'm totally ready and need to start small, in the comfort of our home, before I take bigger steps like going back to school. It's all bullshit. The truth is, I hate that I am ruining everyone's lives.

Finally, Father agrees. "We'll keep it small and short and invite your friends too. And if you get tired, you can go hide in your room. But only if you promise to take me with you. Your mom's friend Lucy can be super annoying." We all laugh, and it's a done deal.

A few hours later, Mother and I are in Dr. K.'s waiting room. Mother pulls the hood of my sweatshirt off my head and touches her hand to my cheek. "I'll sit here and read a magazine," she says. "When you get out we can go have lunch. How about Taco Bell? You always loved it there." She picks up a *Reader's Digest* but doesn't wait for an answer. *You always loved it there.* I have become the past tense.

A few minutes later the receptionist calls my name, and I follow her down a dingy hallway to an office with an open door. Dr. K. is sitting in a big chair.

"Jessie!" She stands up with a huge smile.

She looks different, somehow, outside the hospital. Her hair is pulled up in a bun, and her long skirt makes her look a little Mary Poppins-ish. As much as I wish I was done with head doctors, I'm glad to see her. Obviously, my life is beyond pathetic. Dr. K. walks toward me.

"Is it okay if I give you a hug?" she asks.

I nod and we give each other a quick embrace. Then she gestures for me to take a seat.

I'm disappointed there's no comfy chaise longue where I can stretch out and relax while she tries to get some reaction out of me. There's only a regular gray-metal chair with green padding on the seat and back. The walls of her office are covered in serene nature photos: icebergs, mountain scenes, a close-up of green leaves. Once sitting,

I cross my legs, uncross them, then try to slouch, but that's so uncomfortable I sit up straight again.

Dr. K. laughs. "We need new furniture, I know. That chair is pitiful."

"It's fine," I say. I'm sure most people who sit in this chair have other, bigger things on their minds than interior decorating. Or nothing on their minds at all.

"How are you doing, Jessica?" She leans forward, her brown eyes warm with genuine concern. "I'll bet you've been enjoying the freedom from questions and tests and rehab exercises and all that jazz."

"For sure," I say. "But of course I missed you."

She laughs again. "I know sarcasm when I hear it."

This is friendly chitchat, I know, the warm-up to the real discussion. She's softening me for the tough questions she will soon hurl at me. But if I were to spill my guts now, I would tell her that I missed it all: the smell of the hospital, the sounds of the elevators and meal carts, the dumb exercises in the rehab room, even the grumpy nurses. But then she'd know how nuts I really am.

"But seriously, Jessica"—her tone takes a turn, from *shooting the breeze* to *let's pick your brains* in the nicest way possible—"how has it been, going back home? Has it been what you imagined?"

What I imagined? First real question and she's already got me stumped. I let out a long, intelligent "Uuuuuh" to show her I'm not ignoring her but thinking.

What did I imagine? A week ago already seems like a whole other lifetime, and whatever I might have envisioned for life at home has been replaced by real, fresh images of reality.

"Well," I answer slowly, "it's been all right."

She waits. But the crazy thing is that even if I did want to talk about it, I don't know how I feel. I like being around Stephen. Mother and Father try so hard, and seriously, how could any sane person prefer the hospital? But the problem is, I don't feel like I belong in that house with those people. I'm like an ungrateful guest with no manners.

"It's confusing," I say finally, as Dr. K. peers at me intently. "I want to like it. But mostly it's just weird."

"What is weird, exactly?" Dr. K. loves specifics.

The first thing that pops into my mind is Mother standing beside my bed, asking me if I want to go for a walk. I can feel the heaviness of her expectations as though she were sitting on my chest.

"Everyone wants me to be normal. Or at least try harder to be like the old me. But I don't feel normal at all."

"What's normal to you?"

She, of all people, understands I can't answer that question. I try counting in my head to calm myself, to keep from snapping out something nasty. But she sees right through me.

"You know, Jessica, you can tell me if you don't like a question. But I will probably still want you to answer it.

This whole therapy thing is not going to be easy. But if you give it a chance, it will help you transition more smoothly back to real life."

Real life. Normal. Could someone tell me what those things are? I want to be that Girl they all want me to be, but I didn't exactly get an *Idiot's Guide to Being Your Former Self* when I woke up from my Deep Sleep. But Dr. K. wants an answer. Now.

"All right. Yeah, I don't like the question. How am I supposed to know what real life is or how to fit back in? I'm a bit of a freak, if you haven't already noticed."

Dr. K. frowns. "Please don't call yourself names. I know it's your way of joking around, but you are absolutely not a freak. You are a fabulous, bright, young woman, and you have had something horrible and difficult happen to you."

Her words are like a kick in the side. *Horrible.* Heat rises in my face, and my eyes water. But it is not sadness. I feel like smashing something, hurling nasty words at the universe for what's it done to me. It's true. It is horrible and not fair, and I want to know what I've done to deserve this.

"Actually," I say, "I hate your useless questions. And I hate trying to hold everything in all the time. I hate, hate, hate it!" I stand up and push the cheap, ugly chair so that it lands with a clatter on the floor. My heart is pounding so hard it feels like it will leap out of my chest.

Dr. K. stands up and comes toward me. "It's okay," she says, her voice soft but firm. "I know this is tough." Her hands are on my arms, pushing them firmly to my sides.

"We're here to work things out. You're very brave to do this." She steers me over to her chair and sits me down. She leans close to me, forces me to look into her eyes.

"Jessie, I know you feel everyone wants something from you. But the only thing I want is to help you. And I can, if you let me. I'm going to be giving you some homework assignments, okay? I want you to start by writing a list of ten things that you are grateful for. We are going to try to focus on the positive side of everything as much as we can. You are too strong for self-pity."

I unlock my eyes from hers, and when I look up I see a print on the wall I hadn't noticed earlier. It's a pasture with a rickety wooden fence at sunrise, the misty dew of early morning sprinkled on the grass and hay bales. It reminds me of our farm, and I am hit with a feeling, or more of a *memory* of a feeling: it's peaceful and warm and feels like belonging. Like what home should feel like. I think of the Girl's eulogy, and how she fit so well into her little cocoon of a life. My shoulders sink.

"She was so damn *perfect*," I say.

# The Imposter

I'm finishing my bowl of Captain Crunch and already Stephen is walking around the house with a big feather duster. Father carries chairs out to the deck. Today is the party.

Father gives me a peck on the cheek. "You really up for this? We could cancel, say you were sick or something."

I shake my head. All I have to do is hold myself together for a couple of hours, smile and play nice. I head to my room to get ready, brushing my hair and putting on makeup and trying to get myself psyched for my role. A few distant relatives are coming, plus the Pink Posse and some old friends of the family. Apparently, I only have one uncle, and he lives down south somewhere. My only living grandparent, my mother's mom, lives in a care home and has even more serious mental issues than I do, according to Stephen.

Everyone coming today expects to see their beloved Jessica. But I know something they don't: the Girl is not going to show up. She's pulled a vanishing act and left me as a body double.

The doorbell rings once, then again. Guests are arriving. I look over at the dress on my bed, the floral getup Mother picked out for me on our shopping trip. Maybe Jessie didn't mind dressing this way. Maybe she felt pretty in that sweet Mommy's-girl look. Something of the old Jessie must still be in me, though, because I rise from the chair and slip the dress over my head. Tugging on the bottom of the dress, I stand in front of the mirror and force my mouth into the biggest grin possible.

I practice. "Hi. Oh, hello. Of course! How could I forget you?"

The door pops open and Stephen pokes his head inside. "Hey, Mom's going to have a fit if you don't get your fancy behind down there."

"Do you mind?" I say. "You could at least knock."

He gives himself a mock slap across the face. "Terribly sorry. But can you come already? I'm tired of having my cheeks pinched."

How could I be mad at a goof like that? I nod and step out the door. Stephen grabs my hand and forces me to take my first step down the stairs. Images from home movies play in my mind: me screeching and tossing water balloons at Megan, her pigtails bouncing as she bolts across the lawn; me giving a heart-rending performance of "Hot Cross Buns" on my recorder for my parents' friends; me twirling across the living room in Father's arms, my feet resting on his as he dances a crazy spinning dance. Me, me, me, doing things I don't recall doing. My feet stop at the bottom of the stairs, refusing to move forward into the living room.

"Don't worry," Stephen whispers, "they're all harmless." He guides me gently, his hand on my back, through the doorway.

The harmless people turn out to be three older couples (obviously more Mother and Father's crowd than mine), who hover around an array of appetizers on the coffee table. My pals, the Pink Posse, are hanging out in the corner by the piano, and a few others are out on the deck. Everyone is chatting, but the words fade and stop when they notice Stephen and me in the doorway. Two women glance in my direction and then pretend to be fascinated with the chips and dip, but most of the people keep on looking at me.

"*Hola*," I say. Megan laughs, a little too enthusiastically, and one of the middle-aged women stands up and steps toward me as Mother enters from the kitchen.

"Jessica, hello," the woman declares as she spreads her arms open. I step back a little, but the woman lunges forward and gives me an upper-body squeeze so fast that I have no time to resist. "Gosh, we're happy to see you!" she announces. "And you're as pretty as a picture in that dress."

I pull myself out of her grip, bumping into the wall as I step backward. Then Father is there, smiling. "Must be the good genes," he quips, and the room erupts in laughter.

Mother crosses the room with half a watermelon cut into a bowl; there are chunks of fruit on wooden skewers jutting from it. She places it on the coffee table. "Have a seat, Jess."

I walk past the oldies, who are now ooohing and aaahing over Mother's fruit artistry, and make my way to Father's brown recliner. My friends nod and smile with their matching glossy lips. I'm suddenly ultra-aware of my dress and how obvious it is that it was chosen by a forty-something-year-old and accepted by a teenager with no mind of her own. Their clothes have more edge: there are studs on Cybil's flowing top and on Megan's leather wristband. Kerry's dress is lime green. Their outfits have personality. Mine shows a lack of one. I slide into a chair next to them and try to take a subtle deep breath.

Megan leans over and whispers, "How goes the battle, Jess?"

"I'm losing," I whisper back. But I must look too serious when I say it, because she doesn't laugh. "And Megan, sorry about the cupcake. My bad."

Her face goes pink, and I can tell by the looks the other girls exchange that Megan has told them about the incident. "No big deal," she says. "It's kind of funny, now that I think of it."

"Hey," Cybil adds, "I've wanted to do that for years!" Megan whacks her on the shoulder, and then they are all laughing and I am too, relieved. Maybe it really was no big deal; maybe that's what teenagers are like, off-the-wall and unpredictable.

The girls banter back and forth for a while, teasing each other about stuff I am clueless about. I chuckle every now and then, thinking, I am Jessica, I am Jessica, they're my friends. Stephen and some other boy run around the house screeching, attacking each other with foam swords. I wish I could play with them, but I know today is not the day.

The adults are all laughing and having a grand old time, and it feels like a real party. I'm proud of myself. Go, me, go. I stand up to head over and check out Mother's spread, but Cybil stops me with a tap on the shoulder. "Jessica, I brought something for you." She reaches in her pocket and then places a smooth lump in my hand. When I open my fingers, two beady little eyes gawk up at me from a green body.

Cybil clears her throat. "He's a yoga frog."

I turn the shiny statue around, but he looks like a regular frog to me: legs stretched out behind him, front legs straight down in front.

She leans closer, pointing at her gift. "That's the frog pose. The one you busted a gut over."

This meant something to the old Jessie, and Cybil couldn't possibly know that the new Jessie hates these smug little amphibians. But I am not good at hiding my disdain, obviously, because her face flushes. "It's lame, I know."

"No, no, I like it," I say. The girls are all looking at me, waiting. "Honestly. It's…cute."

I'm such a jerk. All I can think about suddenly is Lucky Charms and how great a bowl of sugary sweetness would taste right now. It might be a social faux pas to eat cereal at a party, though, so I'll have to settle for a cookie. I walk over to the coffee table.

There are a few conversations going on—"Did you see that new sign Rosie put up for the café? It's butt-ugly," and "There was a dead moose off Highway 22 the other day"—but a hush falls over the room as I inspect the platter of squares and cookies. I feel eyes on me as I select a giant chocolate-chip specimen and place it carefully on a napkin. My legs are wobbly, like the carpet has waves, and I have to concentrate to stay balanced.

I remember my promise to my parents: if it's too much, I will go rest. Maybe five minutes in my room is what I need, before I do something humiliating like toss the giant Frisbee of a cookie at someone's head. I bolt up the stairs quickly and lock my bedroom door behind me.

I walk over to the shelves where all the little froggies hang out. My gift from Cybil is still clenched in my fist, and I lift my arm to introduce him to his homies. But when I place him down, a force stronger than myself takes over.

My arm swings out and swipes at the dopey, cutesy frogs, sending them flying from the shelves in different directions. Some land with cracking sounds on the hardwood floors; some land with a thud on the area rug. I could keep going—it would be so satisfying to stomp on the frogs and hurl them at the walls, to go completely ballistic.

But instead, I wrap my arms tightly around myself and take deep breaths. I've held it together at the party, given the family the fun they deserve. It's almost over.

Hands shaking, I pick the frogs up one by one and place them back in their spots on the shelves. Some of them are missing an arm or a leg; one has a cracked head. "Don't tell anyone," I whisper. I check myself out in the mirror—lip gloss is fine, no signs of a mental breakdown—and head calmly back downstairs. Mother comes out of the kitchen carrying a cake, and I sing "Happy Birthday" along with everyone like nothing has happened.

Soon after the cake is gone, guests are standing up to leave and some are already by the door. I walk over to Cybil and give her a one-armed hug. "Thanks for the frog. I love it." She looks so pleased.

More guests put their coats on, and I shake some hands and say, "Thank you all for coming," a big smile on my face. I think about those disfigured frogs up in my room, and how easy it is to play the role of a regular, well-adjusted teenager being friendly at a party. I'm like a serial killer, with body parts in my freezer, hosting a dinner party. No one knows my dirty little secret: I am not at all who they think I am. And, equally creepy, who I truly am is yet to be determined.

As I wave goodbye through the window, a realization slowly sinks in. Dr. K. asked me what I thought normal was, but maybe it doesn't matter. I don't actually have to *feel* normal. All I have to do is fake it.

———

That night while the family sleeps, I sit in the dark with my phone in my hand. There's no one to text, nothing funny or weird anyone has posted on Facebook. I flip through the shots in the camera roll: Megan and the Pink Posse in ski gear, a heart-shaped cake, a coat hanging on a store rack, a sunset...nothing I haven't seen before. But then something I *haven't* seen before: row upon row of tiny photos of the Girl, up close. A long series of selfies.

The background is the monkey poster on the wall behind the bed—the very wall behind me now. I am surprised to see, when I enlarge the thumbnail of the first photo, how different the Girl looks. She's got on dark eyeliner and what could be fake eyelashes, and pink metallic lipstick. A scarf, a deep cherry red, is draped around her neck. From photo to photo, her expression changes from pouting to defiance to an attempt at being seductive.

There are dozens of photos like that, and for some she has moved the scarf so that it covers her mouth like a veil or draped it dramatically around her head.

I have no way of knowing what the photos were for, if she was trying to be artsy or was simply having fun or had an audience in mind—that boy she liked, Harrison?—when she took them. Whatever their purpose, something about them bothers me. Maybe it's the eagerness in her eyes, the sense of desperation. They're so contrived they're almost pathetic. I click on them one by one and hit *Delete*. I'm sorry, Girl, I think, but one day you'll thank me.

# Vive la Liberté

Father's out in the field. Mother's got errands to do and wants me to come. I'd rather have a lobotomy.

I see it in her face: she's scared to leave me alone. I haven't been on my own for more than a few minutes here and there when she's dropping Stephen off somewhere or picking him up. But I must have done an impressive job of acting normal at the party, because she sighs and scribbles a number on a scrap of paper.

"I won't be long," she says. "Call if you need me." But when she is about to close the door, she looks back at me and I see the worry in her eyes. "You sure you don't want to come? We can get slushies."

I have to laugh. "No, thanks. I'll be fine here."

She nods and shuts the door behind her. I wait to hear her car drive away down the road.

Peace. I am alone. My heart flutters with excitement as I stand in the middle of the living room, looking around.

What to do first? Eat chocolate chips for breakfast maybe? Play obnoxiously loud music and jump around on the furniture? Fill the bathtub with Jell-O? Too childish. If that's all I can come up with, I definitely am a lost cause.

Decision: I will start with breakfast. I find a tube of rainbow sprinkles, the kind kids love on cupcakes. I take out an extra-large salad bowl and empty the entire contents of the tube onto some Fruit Loops. Then I grab whatever else in the pantry catches my eye—butterscotch chips, flakes of coconut, chocolate sundae sauce, mini marshmallows—and pour it into the bowl. I add milk, grab a serving spoon and head outside to the tire swing I spotted in the backyard.

Munching on my concoction, I look around at the house and the trees and the clouds floating above. Jessica loved the farm and felt at home here. She was obviously naïve, had no idea that it would all go so wrong so quickly. I picture the scene on the Very Bad Day, the Girl lying injured in the pen. But how did she get there? I squeeze my eyes shut and imagine the Girl, going about a typical afternoon on the ranch.

There she is in her farm clothes, whistling as she walks toward the bison pen, oblivious to the danger lurking ahead. The scene plays out like a movie in my mind, with the Girl in the starring role.

FADE IN:
EXT. PRAIRIE FARMYARD—DAWN

Teenage GIRL, wearing faded jeans, rubber boots and a plaid coat, closes the back door of house. A golden retriever jumps excitedly beside her as she makes her way down a path through tall weeds into a pasture and up to a green tractor RUMBLING and spewing exhaust.

> GIRL
> (cheerfully)
> Hey, Pops.

> FATHER
> (atop tractor)
> Hello, darling daughter. Can you take care of the watering?

> GIRL
> Consider it done.

Girl HUMS as she strolls down a trail winding through birch trees. She approaches a high fence with a metal gate. Girl turns on a spigot, and water SPUTTERS out of a black hose that snakes through the fence and into a trough.

SNORTING sounds are heard, and from the trees inside the fence emerge several bison. They make their way toward the trough.

GIRL

That's right, big fellas. Come wet your whistle.

The beasts push against each other, GRUNTING and drinking from the water with their long pink tongues. The girl watches, grinning. Suddenly, water stops coming out of the hose. She frowns, kicks at the hose. Still no water. She walks over to the spigot and plays with it, but it doesn't work. Peering through the fence railing, she sees that a large rock is sitting on the hose.

GIRL

Shit.

Girl glances at the bison, sighs and then squeezes between the fencepost and the gate. She reaches for the rock, her body halfway into the pen. She can't quite reach it and leans in a little farther.

CLOSE UP

The largest bison, a male, comes out from behind the others. He paws at the ground.

As the girl turns and sees him, he begins to move toward her.

GIRL
(frantically)

Shit!

Girl jerks back, but the bottom of her coat has snagged on the fence. The beast is there, his enormous head low and aimed directly at her. Girl SCREAMS.

FADE TO BLACK.
Sound of ambulance SIRENS.

My eyes pop open, and I flop backward in the swing. End of scene. But not end of story.

The sky is a soft blue, and a black bird circles above me. An idea hits. *Of course.* There is something I should do when no one is around to baby me. I pull my legs out of the tire and put my bowl down in the grass.

It's time to pay Ramses a little visit.

The walk is only a few minutes, back behind Father's shop and past the garden. I move on automatic pilot, marching across the yard before I can change my mind. There's a small dugout surrounded by willows and then a string of barbed-wire fence along a pasture.

No one has told me where the bison are exactly, but I've seen Father walk in this direction, and I trust my body to lead me there.

I wonder if the bison will recognize me, if Ramses has some kind of memory of the terrible thing he did to me, someone who bottle-fed him when he was a baby. I know from photos that he is massive and awe-inspiring now, and I hope he's in a good mood.

I hear the bison before I see them. The sound starts as a grunting so low I can't tell if it's only in my imagination, but the two long, screeching bellows that follow leave no doubt in my mind. I'm getting warmer. My eyes scan the spaces between trees for movement, so I don't see the mudhole until my left foot has sunk right into it. I look down, about to back up, as my right foot lands in a puddle. My jeans are wet to the knee by the time I cross the mud, and I break into a run toward a clearing in the trees. I jump over a fallen willow, my heart hammering in my chest. The sun glistens off the barbed-wire fence ahead of me.

I step into the clearing. To my right, the wire fence line connects to a thick wooden post taller than I am. Branching off the post is an enclosure, a pen about the size of our front lawn, its railing made with thick metal tubing. There's a wide gate at the end, tied with metal chains. The ground inside the pen is rutted and sprinkled with yellow clumps of hay, but there are no animals inside.

But then there is a flash of brown between the fence rails and suddenly one is in plain view: a bison. His dark brown fur hangs in clumps around his enormous head, which is cocked to the side as he glares at me suspiciously. I haven't seen the others, but I know it somehow inside: This is him. Ramses. My friend, my enemy.

"It's all right," I say, my voice shaky. "I come in peace." I slow to a walk and am only a few feet from the fence when I see, behind my observer, a dozen or more of the animals. Some look at me, and the rest graze on the pale grass. I take deep breaths as I approach. Now what?

"Long time no—"

Ramses lets out a loud snort and paws at the earth, shaking his giant head from side to side. And then, in the blink of an eye, he turns to face the herd. The beasts begin to move, slowly at first, and then the ground rumbles as they gallop off into the pasture, clumps of dirt flying in the air around them. I watch their shrinking shapes, panic clutching at me. That's it? I came to face my nemesis, to have some kind of Big Moment, and the beasts are running away?

"Come back here!" I scream. "You owe me this, at least!"

I could run out into the pasture, chase after them and make them pay attention. Crazily, I'm not even scared. Here I am, a broken person because of them, and they're the ones hightailing it out of here.

A snort of laughter escapes my lips, and my shoulders begin to shake. The laugh grows harder, coming from a place somewhere deep inside, until I'm doubled over. I fall to my knees in the muddy earth. Tears, actual tears, stream down my cheeks, and when I reach up to wipe them, my chest cracks with a sob.

How pathetic. I don't know whether to laugh or cry. I am drained and crashing from all the sugar, and all I can think to do is what I do best: go back to my room and bury myself under the covers, wasting away another morning.

# Hellhole

I wake up to the smell of waffles. When I step into the kitchen, Father's standing at the stove, wearing a frilly apron, and Stephen is digging into a mountain of whipped cream on his plate. Mother sits with her hands wrapped around a cup of coffee, eyes puffy. Father sings a song about mamas not letting their sons grow up to be cowboys, shooting smiles and winking at her, but he's not getting more than a hesitant smile in return. I've been holding it together pretty well the last few days, but maybe not enough to stop Mother from worrying late at night.

"I know," Father says suddenly. "Let's go to Mud Bog!"

Stephen leaps out of his chair and does a crazy kind of hip-hop chicken dance. Mother shakes her head, but Father insists that we all need to get ready, because he is kidnapping us.

After a basic hygiene routine upstairs, I slide into the backseat of the truck beside Stephen.

"It's the perfect weather for it too," Stephen says. "Totally perfect." When I ask him what the Mud Thingy is anyway, he merely grins. "You'll see."

Father barrels down the gravel roads until we pass the town's school, a gray concrete block with small windows, and reach a large field with rows and rows of parked cars. A red pickup is parked at the entrance, a couple of teenagers sitting on the tailgate, feet dangling. A tall guy with a shaved head jumps down and saunters up to our window. "Hello, Mr. Grenier. It's twenty for the carload." He leans his head closer to peer into the truck and nods when he spots me. "Hey, Jessica. Good to see you."

"You too," I choke out, but he could be the son of Satan for all I know. I've been so caught up in the mystery of the Mud Bog that I haven't had time to plan a strategy for faking my way through a day out in public.

Father parks the car and Stephen practically leaps out. "Come on," he says, pulling my arm. "What are you waiting for?"

"For a wizard to appear and magically transport me to a parallel universe?" I mumble. But his tugging pries me from the backseat. Mother and Father wait for us, holding hands. A roaring sound comes from a tall set of metal bleachers, and the crowd erupts in cheers.

"The Monster Truck," Stephen squeals. "I've died and gone to heaven." We follow Mother and Father across the field to the grandstand. It's packed with a sea of spectators, and the air smells like gasoline. Some kids around Stephen's age shuffle over, and we squeeze into the bottom row. Stephen's face lights up at the scene before us: a huge truck, wheels taller than our car, gunning it through a pit of mud. It pops up onto its back tires, sludge spraying in every direction, and slides across the pit, then back again. The crowd—including Little Man—goes wild. It's way too loud but still impressive, in a hokey kind of way, so I clap a little.

"And now," a voice booms from a speaker, "some local daredevils will attempt to cross the pit. First, introducing the Angel of Death."

I lean forward to see if I can catch a glimpse of the Angel, but someone tugs on my collar from behind. I glance over my shoulder and am met with a familiar face: dark-purple bangs over eyes circled in heavy black eyeliner, black lipstick and silver hoops in the nose. It takes me a few seconds to place her, outside the hospital and its pale walls, but when I do I can't help smiling.

"Tarin," I say, but I'm barely audible over the hoots of excitement.

She bends forward and says loudly in my ear, "Isn't this lame-ass?"

Stephen elbows me. "Check it out!"

The Angel's jacked-up rusty pickup shoots out from the side of the pit, and he flies through the mud. But less than halfway across, the truck suddenly flips onto its side, and a hush falls over the crowd. The tires spin in the air, and then the door pops open and a head sporting goggles and a helmet appears. Everyone is standing and screaming as the Angel, a big guy with a scraggly beard, climbs out and leaps into the mud.

"He seems to be all right, everyone," says the announcer, and the crowd goes crazy.

Tarin's voice comes in my ear again. "Only he's still a moron."

And it continues like this. Drivers take turns ripping through the sludge in whatever vehicle they've patched together with duct tape. One older guy even attempts the bog on an old ride-on lawn mower, which has the crowd howling with laughter. Tarin shares her scathing commentary with me from behind. On the other side of Stephen, Mother's face is relaxed and happy. She isn't cheering or laughing, but she looks, for once, like she is not thinking. Just being.

Tarin squeezes in beside me, crosses her arms and surveys the pit.

"What a hellhole," she says.

"Hey," Stephen says, "I recognize you. From the hospital, right?"

Tarin nods. "Yeah, that's me. The brilliant surgeon who saved your young and promising sister's life."

Stephen stands up and stretches. "Ha-ha." He turns to Mother. "Can I have some money for an ice cream?"

Mother pulls a bill out of her purse and hands it to Stephen. He bounds off, and Mother looks past me at Tarin.

"Hello," she says. "You're Mrs. Meyer's granddaughter, right? How's your gran doing?"

Tarin surprises me by putting on a making-polite-chitchat smile. "She's home now, but we're sticking around a little longer to make sure she's all right on her own. I think Mom's enjoying the excuse to escape the drudgery of city life for some country living." She winks, and Mother laughs. "Could I steal your daughter for a few minutes? I'm itching to get some ice cream too."

I can see the internal struggle on Mother's face. Tarin might be our neighbor's granddaughter, but she looks like a vampire. Finally, Mother nods and hands me some money. Tarin and I make our way to the wooden booths and get two fudge bars on sticks, then stroll alongside the pit's chain-link fence. We rip off the paper wrappings and lick the creamy treats.

"Divine," she says. And I'm hit with a twang of guilt. I gave her the cold shoulder at the hospital when she came to say goodbye.

"I'm sorry," I say.

She stops mid-lick and looks at me with surprise. "For what, dude?"

"For being a jerk in the hospital."

"Oh, that." She finishes her lick. "I was a little steamed, I have to admit. But then Gran told me later what had happened to you, about your coma and brain injury and all that. Holy crap. How could I be mad at you anymore?"

We've come to the corner of the field, so we turn and continue along the other side. She's the first person I can think of, other than the doctors, who has come right out and said what happened to me, not calling it "the accident" or my "difficulties."

"Well, my apologies all the same. A dent in my frontal lobe is getting to be an old excuse."

She laughs.

"What grade are you in?" I ask. I try to envision her at school, hanging out with Megan and the Posse, but I can't fit the two images together.

"I should be in grade eleven. But since Mom and I have been moving around a bit, I've been taking online courses. Saves me all the hassle of actually sitting in a classroom listening to all that brainwashing. My boyfriend graduated last year, and he says being out in the world is where the real education is. Stuff you can't get from books."

"Cool," I say.

"How's that head of yours anyway?" she asks. "You seem kind of normal."

"Kind of?" I punch her shoulder in fake outrage.

She laughs. "Well, I only know you as damaged goods, you know. I don't have anything to compare you to."

I roll my eyes. "Join the club."

She stops, clutching my elbow, and leans in so close I see sparkly silver flecks in her mascara. "What do you mean?"

I wonder if I've gone too far, if I should let it go and keep it casual. But Tarin doesn't seem like the kind of person who will squirm at the truth.

"I can't remember my life before the accident," I say.

Her eyes open wide, and she lets out a long, deep breath. "For real? So you don't remember anything, like what's-her-name on that soap we watched in the hospital? Felicity or whatever?" She studies me closely, but I don't feel like it's unkind. Only curious.

"Felonia," I say. "Actually, I do remember some things. Bits and pieces, mostly from years ago. But, well…" She's waiting, a trickle of melted fudge bar traveling down her wrist. It dawns on me then that I'm starting from scratch with her. She, unlike everyone else I know, doesn't care one bit whether I go back to being who I used to be. "I don't really feel like I'm the same person. I don't even know who that girl was exactly."

I can't believe I'm telling my biggest secret to someone who is practically a stranger. But I feel lighter, somehow, having said it.

"Whoa," she says. "That's wild." She leans beside me on the fence, and we finish our fudge bars, the sound of revving tractors and the cheering crowd behind us. When we've cleaned the last drops off the wooden sticks, she sighs loudly.

"I thought I had problems," she says. "Man."

We walk back toward the bleachers, and being out too long in the sun hits me all of a sudden. I am tired, so tired, and when Mother sees my face she nudges Father to tell him it's time to go. Tarin says goodbye and tells me to take it easy, and when we're halfway to the truck she runs up behind me and hands me a wooden ice-cream stick with a phone number scribbled on it.

"In case you ever get bored," she says.

Stephen watches her through the window as we pull out of the grounds. "She's weird," he says.

"Yeah," I answer with a smile. "Yeah, she is."

# Ancient
# History

It's past midnight, but the long nap I took after the
Mud Bog has me charged up and ready to watch some
cheesy made-for-TV movies. I am not alone in my rest-
lessness. As I descend the stairs to the basement, I hear
the murmur of the TV. Father sits on the couch, watching
a long wooden boat float across the screen. I clear my
throat, and he turns around.

"Can't sleep either, hey?" He pats the spot beside him.
"Come watch this documentary with me. It's a reenact-
ment of life in ancient Egypt. Pretty amazing stuff."

I sink into the couch as, on-screen, brown-skinned
men in loincloths jump out of the boat and pull it onto
the bank.

"You always loved watching these things with me. They
put your mother to sleep." Father chuckles. The next half
hour is about the transportation methods of the Egyptians
and the role the Nile played in their lives, and though it's

not mind-blowingly fascinating, it does take my mind off little old me, me, me. I feel safe there with him.

When the credits roll, Father yawns and clicks the TV off. He starts to stand up, and before I have time to chicken out, I grab his arm.

"Can you tell me about what happened?"

He freezes in position, half standing, and looks at me, puzzled. "What? What happened—"

But I don't need to answer, because his eyes widen and he slowly settles back into the couch. "Ah," he says. "I see."

"I'm ready to hear the details."

His entire body sags from the weight of my request. "There isn't much that I haven't already told you. But I can try."

We sit there in the quiet, looking at each other, and then he sighs. "I've thought about it a lot, struggled to piece it all together. I thought at first that you fell into the pen, but then I realized you wouldn't have been so far from the fence. But why would you ever go in there on purpose? What could have come over you to make you do something you knew was so dangerous?"

Come over *me*? Doesn't he mean Ramses?

Confusion must be written all over my face, because Father's eyes narrow and he leans closer. "You do mean why did you go in the pen, right?"

A jolt goes through me. "Wasn't I feeding them or something?" I've been assuming all this time that there was a reason I went in the bison pen in the first place. That I was simply being a regular farm girl going about my daily farm business.

Father shakes his head. "We only use the pen for giving them shots or when we need to get them on or off trucks. I feed them with the tractor; watering is done from outside the pen. And they didn't need to be watered or anything that night. You knew that. All I know is I came out of the shop, walked toward the pen and saw you lying there on the ground. I still can't figure it out. You knew the bison well and were always careful around them, knew better than to waltz in there like it was a petting zoo."

All this time I've thought maybe the family was keeping something from me, some horrific detail they didn't want me to hear. But the truth is, they didn't know any more than I did about what went wrong. My head is reeling, and I take long, deep breaths to try to calm my racing heart. Where's that yoga lady when you need her?

Father closes his eyes and rubs his hands over his forehead, as though he is trying to erase the image. "At first, when I saw you lying there, I didn't even realize it was you. You looked like"—he swallows hard—"a rag doll, limbs stretched out at awkward angles. I called your name, louder and louder, as I ran to you. By the time I got to you, I was screaming for help. From whom, I don't know. God maybe?"

I look over at this man who, I know from photo albums, was not only my father but also my buddy, and I sense the strength draining out of him as he talks about what happened. His eyes meet mine, the muscles in his jaw clenching. "When I got close and saw the gash on the side of your head, and Ramses standing there, near the gate, it was like someone punched me in the stomach—hard. The air went right out of me. I opened the gate and Ramses took off into the field to join the others. I held your head in my hands, didn't know what to do. I couldn't move you, knew that might injure you even more. I needed to get help but was terrified to leave you there, alone with the bison. So I screamed and yelled at the top of my lungs, and somehow Stephen heard me and got your mother. The rest is a blur. The ambulance came, and then we spent the night at the hospital, waiting to see if you'd pull through."

A shudder goes through his body. "I don't know if I should really tell you all this. But if I were you, I'd want to know too. So I'll level with you: it was all terrible, every second of it. A parent's worst nightmare. But the very worst was yet to come. All those days you were in the coma, hooked up to machines, we agonized, sitting by your bed, waiting. All we wanted was a sign, a tiny wiggle of your pinkie toe or whatever, to show us you were not going to die."

He chews on his bottom lip before he continues. "And then, finally, good news. You had come out of your coma.

Your mother and I laughed and cried at the same time, we were so happy. We were ready to smother you with kisses and make you promise never to scare us like that again. Then came the part that nearly broke your mother's heart."

"When I didn't remember you?" I say.

His eyes glisten, and he puts his hand on my knee. "No, no, not that. That was hard too, of course. Worse was seeing you sitting in the corner of the room like a scared animal, then reaching to touch you and having you scream and scratch and pull your own hair."

"Is that when I hit Mother?"

His eyebrows lift. "How did you know?"

"Stephen."

His body relaxes now, likely with relief that he has told me and I haven't freaked out on him. "That little turkey."

We sit there and watch the blank TV screen. "You okay with all that?" Father asks. His face looks tired but peaceful, like he's gotten a heavy weight off his shoulders.

"Yeah," I say. "I guess."

"Being a parent is a tough gig sometimes," he says, maybe more to himself than to me. "We don't always know if we're making the right choices. I hope I never let you down."

I shake my head. "You're a great father," I say.

He looks at me with earnest eyes. "I'm a father, yes. But mostly I'm your *dad*."

I nod. "All right," I say. "Dad." And I like the way it sounds.

We stay there, his hand on my knee, until he announces that he needs his beauty sleep and that I should get to bed too. He kisses me on the forehead, then heads up the stairs. I stay in the quiet of the basement and try to let the details sink in: lying in the pen like a rag doll; Father— Dad—screaming; the Girl (or was it me, or neither of us but some other version of this Jessica?), scratching and crazed, head spinning around on her neck like the girl in *The Exorcist.*

Now that I've finally worked up the courage to ask questions, I can pester Dad and Mother and Stephen all I want to give me a second-by-second, play-by-play account of every detail they remember. But I also know now that it will get me nowhere. Because the truth is hiding in one place and one place only: the corners of my own broken mind.

# Rose-Colored Glasses

Stephen and I spend Sunday running around outside, throwing Nerf balls at each other. I'm grateful he is there to take my mind off my chat with Dad and the questions it left me with.

After dinner, though, when Stephen is working on his homework at the kitchen table, they creep into my mind. Why did Jessica go into the pen? How will I ever figure it out when my brain refuses to cough up the memories?

I decide to watch TV, then remember that tomorrow is my next appointment with Dr. K. and I still haven't done *my* homework. I sit at the desk in my room and take out some paper and a pen.

I am *too strong for self-pity*, Dr. K. said. I'm not sure what she meant exactly, but I am going to give this positivity thing a try.

## *10 Things I Am Grateful For*

The first five come easily.

*1. I am grateful that I can walk. And talk. And I don't drool or have to wear diapers like some of the people I saw in the hospital.*

*2. I am grateful that my family has not given up on me.*

*3. I am grateful that my little brother pretends not to notice that he is smarter than me now.*

*4. I am grateful that Ginger doesn't seem to notice that anything has changed.*

*5. I am grateful that Mother lets me eat all the cereal I want.*

Then I am stuck. All that comes to mind is the negative: I've lost my past, I make my friends squirm, I watch too much TV, I sleep too much, my brain doesn't work properly. But I know Dr. K. will not let me get away with doing half the work, so I try to fake one.

*6. I am grateful for my frog collection.*

I eye the pathetic little creatures with their cracks and missing body parts, and I can't lie. I cross it out.

A new number six:

*6. I am grateful that I don't smell bad. Not that I know of anyway.*

I'm totally scraping the bottom of the barrel.

*7. I am grateful for Felonia and Sam and Dr. DiCaprio on* Through the Hourglass. *They give me something to look forward to every day.*
*8. I am grateful for the trees and sky and squirrels.*
*9. I am grateful for naps.*

The last one is only mostly true, but it's the best I can do.

*10. I am grateful that, on that Very Bad Day, Ramses was not pissed off enough to kill me.*

I take stock of the page, doubting this is what Dr. K. is after. But it's all I've got. I open my desk drawer and dig around for an envelope to put it in, but I don't find one, so I head to Stephen's room. His desk is piled high with books and papers and a bunch of magnets, and in the corner there's a framed photo of the Girl and him, hiking sticks in hand. In the top drawer, there are pencil crayons and some LEGO pieces. The next drawer holds construction paper and a plastic bin. I try to pull the bin out, but something is wedged behind it, so I reach in and feel something soft—maybe a sock. A good yank, and the bin slides out of the drawer.

Even though it's partly balled up, I recognize the soft thing from the Girl's weird selfies: it's the bright red scarf she draped over her face and wrapped around her neck. An odd feeling, like I'm holding something the Girl cared about, something private, comes over me. Stephen must have been playing with it or using it to tie up some contraption. As much as I hated those photos, the scarf was hers, and maybe it meant something to her.

I give up on the envelope and shove the scarf in my pocket. Back in my room, I put the scarf where it belongs: in the Girl's shoebox, with all the other mementos of her lost life.

# Spontaneity

This time I ditch the sweats and wear a nice outfit to see Dr. K.: a short denim skirt and a green jacket with guitar-shaped buttons. She whistles when I walk into the room.

"Hello, gorgeous," she says, and I feel myself blush.

I settle into the metal chair, and she asks me if I did my homework. I read her the list of things I am grateful for, and she nods and smiles. "Nice job. Try making that a regular thing, and finding the positive side will become more natural. For next week, I'd like you to try something a little different. I want you to write a letter to your pre-accident self."

"Letter?" I say. "To say what?"

"Whatever you want. What do you think?"

I shrug. "You're the doctor."

Then she leans forward in her chair, and the dreaded question comes. "So, how are things? How was real life this week?"

Take it question by question, I tell myself, and keep breathing. She's here to help.

"Well," I say, "lots of things happened, I guess. We had a party."

"How'd that go?"

I decide to be honest. "I kept it together mostly. I did freak out a little, but alone in my room."

She nods. "Mmmm. And have you ever thought of maybe talking to your parents, telling them why you're freaking out? I'm sure they'd listen."

She has a point. It hasn't actually occurred to me to turn to them when I'm coming undone. But don't they have enough to deal with already?

"I guess," I say. "Oh, and I went to see the bison."

"Wow." She scribbles in her notepad. "That was brave."

I shrug. "Not really. They just ran away."

"Sounds like an all-right week," she says. "Any disappointments?"

I should have known she wouldn't let me just scratch the surface. I think of Dad in the basement, and all those questions that are floating around in my head now. "I found out some things about the accident," I say. "Like, no one knows why I went into the bison pen in the first place."

Dr. K. sits up straight. "Is that right? I didn't know that either. Is that bothering you?"

A long sigh comes out of me, and I know I can't lie. "Yeah. I have no idea how to figure out what happened. If I never remember…"

And it's there, suddenly, hanging in the air between us, the thing no one wants to talk about. What if my memories never come back? Could I be stuck like this, in limbo, for the rest of my life?

"Well," she says, her voice softening, "you will probably remember more of your past with time. But it is possible you will never remember the details of that day exactly. Are you prepared for that possibility?"

Frustration flickers inside my chest. But I don't want to be like that today. I want to stay thinking positive, try not to dwell on the black hole that has sucked up my life. I look her straight in the eye, clear my throat and decide to take a leap.

"I want to go back to school," I say.

# Need for Speed

D r. K. talks to Mother after my appointment, and arrangements are made for me to spend a morning at school.

But until then, there are more days to kill at home. Mother asks me to help with some cleaning, but I say I'm tired and hide in the basement to watch my soap. Hot doctor DiCaprio has proposed to Felonia. She tearfully accepts. Brain damage seems to be the best thing that ever happened to her.

I flip through the Girl's photo albums yet again. There's a photo of Stephen and me cruising down the driveway in ATVs. A mini Mud Bog. I pull it out of its little transparent sleeve and slip it into my pocket. Later, I fall asleep on the couch and wake up to Stephen shaking my shoulder. He plunks down on the floor.

"It's nice out," he says. "Wanna do something?"

Maybe it's out of pity for his pathetic couch-potato sister, but whatever. I'll take what I can get.

"Yeah." I sit up, pull the photo out of my pocket and show it to him. "This."

His lips turn up in a small smile. "Quadding? You really think they're going to let us?"

Our parents are nowhere to be found in the house, so we slip on our rubber boots and head outside. The door to Dad's shop is open, and when we step through the doorway, Dad has his arms around Mother, her face buried in his shoulders. He sees us and pulls away. "Hey," he says, and Mother swipes her cheeks before looking over at us. I can imagine the conversation we interrupted. *School? Can she possibly be ready for school?*

Stephen pretends not to notice the awkwardness. "Can Jessie and I take a spin on the quad?"

Dad looks over at Mother. "I don't know," he says. "That seems a little soon."

"Please!" Stephen begs. "We'll go super slow and wear our helmets."

Dad sighs. "Well, only if you ride with Stephen, Jessie. You need to take it easy for a while." Mother doesn't look enthused but must be too drained to fight us. She shrugs.

Little Man and I high-five each other and head outside. He points at a smaller building. "Go grab some helmets."

In the shed, there are bikes and skis and all kinds of sports equipment. Hanging on hooks are helmets of different sizes and colors. I grab a red helmet that looks like it would fit Little Man and a bigger one for me, then find Stephen outside the shop, dusting off the black seat of a yellow quad. All this must be exciting Ginger, because she wags her tail so hard it thumps loudly against the gas tank.

"Jess," Stephen says, "those are ski helmets!"

"Right," I say. "I knew that."

He shrugs. "Minor detail." Pulling on the red helmet, he slides onto the seat. When he turns the key in the ignition, the machine shakes to life. It's loud, and exhaust pours out the back. Stephen's goofy grin under the shiny helmet makes me laugh.

"You know how to drive this thing for real?" I ask. "Aren't you a little young?"

He rolls his eyes. "Duh. We're farm kids. Hop on," he says. I put my helmet on and slide in behind him. "And hold on!" My hands on his shoulder, he revs the engine, and the machine lurches forward, sending our helmets clinking together.

We motor down the driveway, and the noise, the bumpiness, the breeze on my face all take me back to another day and another quad ride. *My hands, smaller then, twisting the handlebars in anticipation. "Now take it easy, my girl," Dad says from behind me. "This one's got more power than you're used to." I nod, but the moment my thumb hits the gas, the quad leaps forward like a wild beast released from a chute. I screech with laughter. I push the brake and jerk to a halt, and when I turn around, there is Dad, lying in the tall grass beside the road. My heart thumps, but as soon as he sits up and glares at me with a crazy grin, I know he's all right. "Wild thing," he says. "You almost killed me!"*

"This too fast?" Stephen yells over his shoulder, and I am back in the present.

"God, no! I'm falling asleep back here."

"You asked for it," he says, and we are off, really off, this time. He drives faster, not fast enough to scare me but enough that I have to wrap my arms around his waist to hold on. We peel out of the driveway and onto the gravel road. It feels amazing—the wind sending tears out of the corners of my eyes, the sun hot on my face, the sound of the machine and the jolts as we hit ruts. Now this is country living. We rip to the stop sign at the end of the road and skid to a stop.

The road beyond the stop sign is muddy and wet, and the only way to avoid it would be to head down the steep ditch. Stephen revs the engine and drives straight into the mud, sending a huge spray of brown water shooting off both sides of our vehicle. We scream, the two of us, a long, happy, ode-to-the-universe-and-mud-puddles yell. The quad slips and slides from side to side, then lurches to a stop. Stephen lets out a whoop.

"That was the best!"

"Yeehaw!" I yell.

We're dirty and wet and acting like hillbillies, but it's the most fun I've had in my new life so far. I look around at the fields to either side, the sky stretched out above us. There's nothing but hay bales and a bee buzzing by. I poke Stephen in the ribs.

"My turn," I say.

His head whips around, and he glares at me. "Are you nuts? You heard what Dad said."

"Come on." I gesture around us at the emptiness. "Who's going to know?"

"I will," he snaps, "and you will. Isn't that enough?" He turns back around fast, before I can get a look at his face. But he's sitting straighter, tense, and I wonder if he's about to cry or something. Either he's more of a stickler for rules than I thought, or there's something deeper going on in that high-functioning brain of his.

"Yikes," I say. "You need to chill out."

Stephen gives the quad gas suddenly, and my head jerks back a little. We head down the road toward home. Stephen parks at the end of the driveway, then jumps off and removes his helmet.

He lifts his finger slowly, and I think he's going to give me a lecture on ATV safety or something, but instead he points to the front lawn.

"Who," he says, "is that? And what's she doing?"

For a millisecond I think he's trying to lighten the mood by pretending he sees a Pygmy or something dumb like that. But there's a woman—a real woman in a puffy pink jacket—pounding a white sign into our lawn.

The sign leans slightly to the side, so she straightens it and hammers it one more time, extra hard. The words across the front are bright and red, and I nearly fall off the quad in surprise. *FOR SALE.*

# Penance

Stephen and I are striding across the lawn toward the woman with the sign, and I'm ready to tell her to get off our property, that she's got the wrong place, when Mother comes jogging up behind us.

"Kids," she says. "Wait."

When we turn toward her, she reaches out and grabs us each by a hand. One look at her flushed face, and I know: this woman in the puffy coat does not have the wrong place. Something big is going on.

"Can you guys go in the house for a bit?" Mother's voice wavers. "I'll come talk to you in a few minutes."

Stephen pulls his hand away and plants his hands firmly on his hips. "What's going on? Why does that sign say *for sale?*"

Mother closes her eyes for a second, then lets out a long breath. "Dad and I were going to talk to you tonight. The realtor was supposed to come tomorrow.

Please go in the house, and I'll explain as soon as she leaves."

"Hello!" The woman is calling and waving. "How does this look?"

"This is a joke, right?" Stephen's voice is loud, on the verge of hysterical. "This isn't really happening?"

Mother waves at the woman, then leans closer to Stephen and speaks quietly. "I'm sorry, Stephen. I understand why you're upset. But your dad and I honestly think this is the best decision for the family."

I see a look in Stephen's eyes so intense I'm scared he's going to do something rash. So, for once, I decide to be the reasonable one. I let go of Mother's hand, grab Stephen's and give a gentle tug. "Come on. Let her talk to the realtor. We'll go inside and have a cookie or something." Mother shoots me a grateful look as I lead Stephen across the lawn and inside. We sit at the kitchen table, but neither of us makes a move to get a snack.

Stephen leans his face into his hands. "I can't believe it," he says. "Where are we going to move? I've lived here my whole life."

I'm trying to be the strong one, to keep it together. But though I can't say I have the same attachment to this place, it is where most of my memories are. If we leave, how will I ever get them back?

"Maybe they have a good explanation," I say. "Maybe we're going bankrupt." I think about Mother's weary face when we walked in on them in the shop,

Dad comforting her. Maybe her stress wasn't about me after all.

We sit there staring at the tabletop, the only sound the hum of the fridge. I stand up to get a cookie as the front door opens. Our parents are talking quietly to each other, probably planning their strategy for dealing with mutiny. They step into the kitchen and sit at the table with us. They both have the same expression, a mix of concern and determination. They have some convincing to do. Mother places her hand on Stephen's back, but he shrugs it off.

"We're sorry you had to find out this way," Dad says. "We meant to tell you tonight, to prepare you a little."

Stephen's head shoots up, and his lips are tight with anger. "Tell us? Why couldn't you ask us what we thought before you made such a big decision? We live here too, don't we?"

Dad nods slowly. "We thought about doing that. But honestly, we knew you would never agree to this, even though we believe it might be better for everyone."

"How? How can leaving be better?" Stephen asks.

Mother watches Dad, letting him do the dirty work. "To be frank," he says, "this farm is not making much money. It never has. I love it too. Really, I do. But an old friend is moving back to Winding Creek, and he wants to open a hardware store. He's asked me to go in on it with him. If we sell the farm, we'll have the money to put into starting the business and to maybe buy a house near town."

"What about the bison?" I say.

Dad gazes down at his hands, and his voice softens. "I'm not sure I feel the same way about them anymore." He looks at me, and I'm surprised to see his eyes are damp. "Maybe I trusted them too much before, and it's time to move on."

Mother reaches across the table and lays her hand gently on top of Dad's. "But we want you to know that this is not a sure thing. We still don't know where we'll move exactly. We only wanted to see if there's any interest."

There's a long, heavy silence until Stephen stands up suddenly. "This was your idea, wasn't it?" he says, pointing at Mother. "I bet you're so happy to be finally getting out of here. You've never liked the farm. You're being selfish, and it isn't fair!" He pushes his chair hard so it hits into the table, then storms out of the kitchen and up the stairs. I flinch when his bedroom door slams.

Mother rubs her temples, her eyes closed.

"I'm sorry, Jessie," Dad says. Was this what he was thinking about that night in the basement when he said he hoped he would never let me down?

I don't even know what to say. "All right," is the best I can come up with.

I disappear to my room too, where I collapse on my bed and hide under my pillow. I try to have a nap but only toss and turn. I sit up and put my ear against the wall I share with Stephen. He's playing rock music instead of his usual classical. I get up and knock on his door until he cracks it open a few inches and peers out at me.

"I'm so mad," he says, "I could scribble on the walls or something."

He lets me in, and I sit at his desk while he perches on the edge of his bed. "This is crazy," he says. "Unbelievable."

"Stephen," I say.

"Yeah?" His glasses have slid down his nose a little, and when he looks at me with those pale eyes, a pang shoots right through my heart.

"This isn't Mother's fault," I say.

He keeps looking at me, and suddenly his intelligent eyes unnerve me.

"It's mine," I say.

Still no response. Just that look.

"You know, for what I did."

I want him to say something—anything—maybe argue with me and say it was all an accident, what happened that Very Bad Day. That I shouldn't beat myself up over it. Or maybe say, "That's all right," even if he doesn't totally mean it.

But he doesn't argue and he doesn't try to make me feel better. In fact, there's something hard in his expression, a kind of maturity I haven't seen before. He pushes his glasses back into place. "So, what are you going to do about it?"

What can I say to that? If I had a magic wand, I would wave it and erase everything that happened on that Very Bad Day. I'd fix my brain to good as new and return us all to the Good Old Days. But he's looking at me so intensely, I know this is no time for sarcasm.

"I'll talk to Dad," I say.

# Lying Eyes

When Mother knocks on the door at 7:00 AM, I wish more than anything that I hadn't opened my foolish mouth and asked to go back to school. I waited up half the night for Dad to come home from his buddy's farm, where he was helping with calving, so I could keep my promise to Stephen. But I fell asleep before he got back, and now I have to psych myself up for the biggest test yet: a morning at Winding Creek School.

Buses are lined up outside the school when we arrive, and herds of kids and teenagers with backpacks mill around, laughing and chasing one another. I clench the door handle, and my heart pounds so hard I can feel it in my fingertips. Stephen pops out of the backseat and trots off to the school building.

"I'll walk you in," Mother says.

I don't argue. I don't think I can make it across the parking lot without someone to lean on. Mother can tell how messed up I am, because she opens the door for me and pulls me out of the seat. "It'll be fine," she whispers. "You've been through a lot, and you can do this."

"I can't—" I croak, but she doesn't let me finish. She leans closer, and the bossy tone in her voice that I usually detest sounds beautifully assertive at this moment. "Yes. Yes, you can."

So I put one foot in front of the other and let her lead me toward the front doors. The crowd is thinning out as the students make their way inside, but I've caught the attention of a few groups as we pass. Some kids stare, and some turn to a friend and whisper. Probably something like "Here comes Brain-Dead Girl!"

But I keep my composure, miraculously, and even beat Mother to pushing the heavy doors open. Standing right there, with a stack of books in her arms and that killer smile, is Megan. Queen Supreme of the Pink Posse. Or whatever they call themselves now.

Relief washes over Mother's face. "Thanks, Megan." And I realize then that this is planned, that Mother has called for backup.

"My pleasure, Mrs. Grenier. Hi, Jessie. We're all pumped that you're here."

I nod, and then Mother says goodbye. "It'll be fine," she says. "Megan will take care of you."

My BFF leads me down the hall by the elbow, and the people we pass smile at me, maybe a little too much. Mr. Swanson, the biology teacher, gives me a half hug before

Megan and I take our seats at the front of the class. I try to concentrate on what he's talking about—photosynthesis, ATP, chlorophyll, blah, blah, blah—but my head starts to ache. I look around the room, trying to spot something familiar. When I glance at the back row, my eyes land on a guy with dark hair. I look away quickly, warmth rising in my face.

It's Harrison. The guy from my photos, the one Megan said I was in love with. I make some scribbles in my notebook for a few minutes, then slowly and casually look back in his direction. He's looking down, writing. His neck is long and lean, and his hair falls over his eyes. I imagine myself touching those dark locks, and I feel a little light-headed.

Could it be that I still like him, that somewhere in the back of my mind that old crush is still buried among all the bits and pieces of my past? Or maybe the Girl and I finally have something in common: our taste in guys.

It takes all my self-control not to gawk at and study every inch of him. I focus all my brain cells I've got on Mr. Swanson's notes on the board—about chloroplast, the epidermis, vascular bundles and other such gripping stuff—and then the bell rings, and everyone bolts out of their desks like they got an electric shock. Megan guides me to our lockers.

"I can break into yours if you want," she says. "You've been using the same combo since forever." She laughs. I lean against the locker and close my eyes.

"Hey, babe, you all right?" Megan asks. I open my eyes and nod. "Now we've got gym. We're building a survival shelter outside today. You up for that?" Again I nod.

She opens my locker, we put our bio books away, and then I follow her down the hallway and outside to the soccer field. We're the first ones out there, but two guys in baseball caps walk up behind us. When the taller one smiles at me, my stomach does a flip. It's my dream man. Megan hooks arms with me and squeezes.

"Greetings, gentlemen," she says. "What's the deal with the shelters again?"

"Mr. McCain's going to divide us into groups. Guys against girls. Make it a competition to see who's best fit for surviving in the wild," the shorter guy says.

"Man," Harrison says, "we are going to kick your butts. Like you ladies could make it five seconds without your hairspray and bunny slippers!"

He's only teasing, I know. But I pictured my perfect guy more…intelligent. Sensitive maybe. Those dimples are cute though. Megan gives him a friendly whack on the arm. "Whatever," she says. "You guys would be calling for pizza in fifteen minutes."

We all laugh. Other students are starting to stream out onto the field, and one girl is shrieking and running after some guy who swiped her hat. High school: it's all about the flirting. Apparently, I was a little shy before. Now I feel like a weird, overly jumpy zombie.

Harrison's friend steps closer to me, his green eyes intense. "How are you doing anyway?"

"Fine, thanks," I say. I have a feeling it might be a little awkward if I spill the details of my cereal addiction and fondness for caffeine pills or the status of my anger-management therapy. I need to be casual, have fun. Harrison looks our way, and our eyes meet. He doesn't flinch, but holds his gaze straight on me. My cheeks are getting warm when squeals behind me break the spell.

It's the other members of the Pink Posse. Cybil and Kerry leap on me, giving me hugs. I let them. "Finally! You're back!" Cybil says. "My God, this is so amazing. And you're coming to the pit party on Saturday, right?"

"*Pit* party?"

Kerry laughs. "It's at the gravel pit, the one by the old cemetery. You've got to come."

"I can pick you up," Megan says. "Finally got my driver's."

I shrug, and when I glance toward Harrison, he's still watching me.

I may be brain-damaged, but not so badly that I can't tell when someone's checking me out. Did he and the Girl ever hook up? Did she ever let on that she was into him? I need to grill Megan for information later.

Mr. McCain shows up, a short guy with way too much energy. In five minutes he has us in teams, guys versus girls as predicted, and we've got sheets of plastic, balls of twine and instructions to go into the woods and gather branches to build the best shelter we can. Megan, Cybil, Kerry and I trot toward the trees.

"Let's go over there," Kerry says, pointing to the far end of the soccer field, near the goalpost. "Get away from the crowd."

We follow her, Megan dragging along the roll of plastic. "Find the biggest branches you can," she says. "To build the frame."

The forest floor crunches under our feet as we walk, and I kick at the fallen branches to test their solidity. Some are half-rotten, but I pull the good ones up and drag them to the edge of the bush in a growing pile. It's satisfying, this physical work, so much better than being in a classroom. Our spot is getting a little picked over, so I push deeper into the bush, scanning ahead for good stuff. I'm fired up to beat the guys, to show them we're not pampered sissies.

There's a prime-looking log a bit farther in, so I head that way. I see flashes of clothing through the tree trunks and hear laughing. I make it to the log and sit on it to test it out. Thick and heavy, it's perfect for a solid shelter, but I can't drag it out of there by myself. Back in the direction of the soccer field, I catch a glimpse of Harrison's red baseball cap, so I crouch close to the ground.

Attraction or not, I am not ready for a tête-à-tête in the woods. I'm not even wearing lip gloss.

"Dude." A male voice carries from nearby, amid the trees. I suck in my breath. "Over here. I think we're ready to start building."

Harrison walks toward the voice, and then his buddy comes into view. I sink as low as I can and sit perfectly still.

"Yeah, probably," Harrison says. "Let's make this thing stellar. We've got to win, or we'll never hear the end of it."

Harrison's friend picks up another branch and heaves it onto his shoulder. "What'd you think of Jessie? She looks good, hey?"

"Yeah, she does," Harrison answers. "Really good. Normal, I'd say."

I smile. A girl will take whatever compliment she can get.

"I can't believe she was in a coma, like, only a month ago. Crazy shit."

"Do you think it's true?" Harrison says. I suck in my breath and steady myself on the log.

"What, the coma? I think that'd be pretty hard to make up."

Harrison clears his throat, then spits on the ground. "No, bonehead. I mean the amnesia thing. She looked at me like she knew me."

"What are you saying? That she's faking? Why would she do that?"

It's quiet for a second. "Whatever, man. Forget it. Let's go kick some ass."

They're off, carrying branches for their man cave. And I sit there, shocked and unmoving, my fingernails digging deep into the log.

I am a total moron. My dream man wasn't checking me out at all. He was doubting my performance. A twig snaps behind me, and I turn to see Megan walking toward me. When she gets closer, she offers me a hand.

"Did we tire you out?" she asks, but she doesn't wait for an answer. She pulls me up from the log.

"We need you!" she says. "The guys are in the lead." She practically drags me through the woods, back to the field.

I'm seething, humiliated, and Megan's frantic energy pumps me up even more.

Faking? I'll show that jerk.

My heart races while we drag the branches to our spot, tie them together with twine into a teepee shape and hang plastic sheets on the sides. The boys call to us as they build, saying we are welcome to come and seek shelter when ours falls apart, that in phase two they're going to add a hot tub. Cybil gives them the finger, but they laugh, taking it as the spirit of competition.

"Whoa, you're on fire," Kerry says as I yank and pull at a plastic sheet, trying to get it to fit perfectly. "I'd want you with me any day in the wilds."

Megan, though, has finally clued in that something is off. She looks me in the eye. "You all right?"

I nod and tug harder, and suddenly there's a loud creaking sound. I reach up to the point of our teepee, but it's too late: the twine has come untied, and our frame is tilting to one side. Kerry screeches and tries to hold it together, but everything comes down in one dramatic crash. We stand there, helpless, staring at our hard work turned into a pile of plastic and wood.

Applause erupts across the field, and Harrison's buddy yells, "Yes!"

Megan is watching me, and I can imagine what Mother has told her: *She doesn't handle stress well; she might lash out in anger; she's unpredictable.* My body is almost vibrating, so I take deep breaths and count to ten in my mind as we take stock of the rubble of our shelter. Kerry lifts the biggest branch, struggling to prop it back up, but Megan's eyes stay on me.

She grabs my arm and pulls me aside. "What's going on?" she says. Kerry and Cybil are frantically picking up the pieces of our shelter, yelling directions at each other.

I don't answer, but she leans in closer. "You could always tell me everything, Jess. I know you. You look pissed."

She's right, and even if she doesn't know the Me of right now, Mother has told me that Megan has been my best friend since kindergarten. Maybe it's time I let her in. "Harrison," I say. "He thinks I'm faking."

Her eyes open wide. "What? Seriously? That's ridiculous. You want me to talk to him?"

"No!" I say, a little too loudly.

Kerry glances our way. She and Cybil have the shelter halfway up and are retying some of the branches.

Our faces must show that Megan and I are in the middle of a serious chat, because Kerry doesn't ask us to pick up the slack.

"No," I whisper. "I want to punch his lights out, but I don't want to make a scene. He's a royal asshole, and I was obviously an imbecile for ever liking him."

Megan glances in the direction of Harrison's team. They are sitting cross-legged inside their shelter, pretending to smoke pipes made out of sticks.

"Well," she says, "don't get too worked up about it. He's a good guy, actually."

They're only words, but it feels like she's punched me in the gut—hard. Worked up? Good guy? And she's supposed to be my best friend? My expression obviously says it all, because she reaches for my arm, talking fast. "Dumb thing to say, for sure. You should be mad, of course. But sometimes we don't know how to act around you, Jess. We're trying our best."

Dr. K. would be proud, I think, when I say, in what I hope sounds like a calm voice, "I'm going home now." And I walk away across the field, toward the school doors.

# Part III:
# SURRENDER

*Man stands in his own shadow
and wonders why it's dark.*

—Zen Proverb

# Pen Pals

I sit on a chair outside the principal's office and wait until Mother comes marching down the hall toward me, her face scrunched in worry.

"What happened?" she asks. "Are you okay?"

I shrug and follow her to the car. As we pull out of the parking lot, she sighs loudly a few times. "Seriously, Jessica. Are you going to tell me what's going on?"

"It's no big deal," I say. "I got tired." She doesn't look convinced, but when we get home she doesn't stop me from heading straight to my room.

I am living a lie, trying to pretend to be someone I am not. And when I think I understand the Girl even a little, I get it wrong. This guy, Harrison. How could she like such a jerk? I stand in the middle of the room and look around at all the things the Girl chose to put here: the books, the posters, the fuzzy pillows. What I see on the shelves catches me by surprise.

All those little frogs I smashed on the night of the party look fine, staring up at me like nothing happened. I step closer and study the fine cracks and the clear blobs of glue keeping the damaged parts together. Whoever fixed them must have spent hours. I should be touched. But somehow I'm not convinced they did it for me, exactly—more for the Girl or the memory of her.

I'm living in a museum dedicated to a beloved daughter, sister and friend. One who no longer exists. I march over to the mirror and stare the Girl down.

"You," I say. "Who are you anyway? I'm getting tired of all this. Can't you help me out a little?"

She peers back at me, and I detect a slight twinkle in her eyes. I lean closer, shaking a finger. "You're not faking, are you? Like Harrison said? You wouldn't hide from me on purpose?"

No answer and no reaction. I could reach out and smack that face, punch the glass until it shatters into pieces. But what's the point? I've been down that road, and it never brings me any closer to understanding her. I get so close to the glass that my breathing makes a small circle of fog. "Are you even listening to anything I say?"

And it hits me all of a sudden how this would look if someone saw me talking to my reflection. Totally demented. But then again, Dr. K. did ask me to write the Girl a letter. Is that really any different?

"Fine," I say to the Girl, backing up. I swipe the haze from the glass. "I'll write to you then. You better read it!"

I walk over to my desk and pull out a sheet of paper and a pen.

*Dear Jessie,*
*Hi.*

I chew the end of the ballpoint pen. What is it I want her to know, exactly?

*You don't know me, but I am the new you. The person who has taken over your life.*

As soon as I put ink to paper again, my hand picks up speed, the ideas coming without any thinking at all.

*I feel awkward writing this, and to be honest I don't see the point, but hey, I have to do my homework.*
*I'll cut to the chase. I'm getting pretty frustrated with you. You know everything I need to know, but you are not letting me in at all. What happened on that Very Bad Day? Why did you go in the bison pen when you knew you weren't supposed to? Why did you get us in this fix? It doesn't sound like something you would do, breaking the rules like that.*
*Deep down, though, I don't blame you. Really, all I want is to know you.*
*How are you? Are you lonely where you are? Where are you anyway? Do you feel trapped, like there's a huge wall blocking you, keeping you out? Do you watch me screwing*

*things up and wish you could jump back in and take control? I bet you do. Cause I am seriously a mess.*

*Everyone wants me to be you, but I'm not. The crazy thing is, I don't feel like you, but I'm not me either. I guess I'm nobody. I'm truly sorry that you've been replaced by such a nobody.*

*Things are not so great here in your life. I don't know if you used to like being here. Probably you did. Because you got to choose your friends and what you did and where you went and what you wore and what you put in your room. Not me. I've shown up here, and I have to live with the choices you made and pretend to like it all. Well, most of it is lame. No insult. I'm sure it was all fine for you, but to me it's pure fluff.*

*More than anything, I wish you would come back and take over. Just slip back into this body and start being your-self, and everyone would be so happy. Yeah, they would say, that dumb cow is gone. You're back! Our nice normal sweet Jessie. No more temper tantrums and messy room and hanging out on the couch all day.*

*Trying to be you is a real bitch.*

*Love,*
*Your new self*

I read the letter once, then again. It felt sort of good to write it, but where does it leave me? It's not like the Girl is actually going to write me back.

# Snapping

Stephen does not tell his usual jokes at dinner, nor does he fill us in on his science experiments. He nibbles at his spaghetti until Dad asks me how my first day of school went.

"I survived," I say.

"So you get to take the bus with me now, right?" Stephen asks.

I shrug and he looks back at me, confused. The poor kid is still reeling from the farm being up for sale. I don't have the heart to tell him that we won't be going to school together anytime soon either.

After loading the dishwasher, we all sit in the living room watching TV, but the mood is somber. I feel like I'm suffocating. "I need fresh air," I say, and I march to the front closet and grab my coat. I open the door and step onto the front steps, letting the door swing shut behind me.

The air is slightly cool and filled with the musky smell of fresh-cut wood—Dad must have been cutting logs for the fireplace. I whistle, and Ginger comes scurrying to my side. She rubs against my leg and looks up at me with her soft brown eyes.

"Hey, girl," I say.

A ding comes from my pocket, and I find a new text on my cell. Sorry about today. Please call me. It's Megan. No way am I ready to forgive her yet.

I reach down and rub Ginger's ears. "You love me, don't you?"

Her tongue tickles when she licks my hand. Now this is a real best friend.

"All right, all right. Take it easy." I step off the deck and she trots ahead of me, picking up a stick on the lawn and bringing it back to me. Squirrels chatter in the trees, and an airplane hums in the distance.

I'm probably overreacting with Megan. But I didn't expect that she would actually *defend* Mr. Hot Shit Harrison. I am here now, though, and I'm not going to waste my time thinking about them. Mother and Dad have said that Jessica loved being outdoors, connecting with nature or whatever. And in that eulogy she wrote, she talked about being a country girl at heart. Maybe if I give it a chance it can put me in a happy place too.

I breathe deeply and look around at the trees and the endless sky, and at Ginger sitting at my feet. What made the Girl love this place so much? Was it the crazy squirrels diving from branch to branch, the wisps of cloud above the treetops, the smell of the air?

"It doesn't matter," I say out loud. "Live in the now."

I'm starting to sound like a shrink.

An idea comes to me. Maybe I can take my own photos, add to the Girl's albums or maybe even hang a few on the wall. Things seen through my eyes, not hers. I click on the camera icon on my phone and walk toward the pines, holding the phone in front of me to see the world on its screen. Every few steps I pause to admire the framed art I've created: branches jutting out into the sky, clumps of moss. Halfway into the strip of trees lining the backyard, something grabs my attention. A weathered picnic table, sitting forgotten among the pines, enters my little oblong world. Before I have a chance to think about it, my finger pushes the button and a soft *click* breaks the stillness.

I walk over to the table, brush aside the leaves on the seat and sit down. My photo of the picnic table is somehow better than the real thing—there's nothing else to detract from it, no world to swallow it up and make it invisible.

It's only a pathetic piece of yard furniture, I know, but my throat feels tight, like I might cry. A squirrel chatters above me, sending me leaping up from the table, and I laugh out loud.

"Lunatic," I say—about myself, not the squirrel.

I turn my lens toward the tree branches, the sky, everything around me, and click away. I take photo after photo, of birds and squirrels and branches and clouds and Ginger, until my arms grow tired. I shut off my phone and breathe in the air. Maybe the Girl was on to something with that nature kick of hers.

Ginger puts her soft head in my lap, and a beautiful mellowness surrounds me. My head feels heavy, so I close my eyes and rest it on the tabletop. My breathing grows deep. In my mind I see birds swooping. And then a voice comes in my head.

*"Isn't it incredible?"*

A scene tiptoes into my mind, like someone tapping me on the shoulder and gently turning me around to see.

*I am in a long hall that opens up into high glass ceilings. At the end of the vast room is a stone building with ancient-looking columns rising at its sides. "Amazing," a soft voice says, and I turn to see a man, camera hanging from his neck, standing beside me. He wears a red plaid shirt and jeans, and his face is flushed with excitement. He has a beard, but I know who it is: it's Dad.*

*"Can we go in?" I say, and he smiles.*

*"Of course, of course," he says. "It's like taking a step back in time, thousands of years." We stroll toward the building, and as we get closer I see that another building, also faded a dusty gray, lies on the other side. "The Temple of Dendur." Dad's voice echoes off the walls. "All the way from Egypt."*

*"Wow," I say and step through the columns.*

A loud chatter makes my eyes pop open, and when I sit up there is a squirrel right there on the edge of the picnic table, looking at me. Ginger perks up too and growls, sending the squirrel scurrying off the table and up the trunk of a tree.

I wish I could go back to the memory, just close my eyes and transport myself to that room, that day with Dad. But the spell is broken.

"That was so real," I say to Ginger. "And"—it sinks in as I'm saying it—"not very long ago, I think." I rub her ears and she looks up at me, her eyes so expressive I could swear she understands.

This is a pretty big deal. A recent memory. Everything else up to now—what little there has been—has been childhood stuff.

"Jess?" Mother calls. "You okay out there?"

I shove the phone into my pocket and stroll back to the house. Mother holds the door open for me. "Megan called," she says. "She's been trying to reach you on your cell." I nod and make my way up to my room, where I sit on the bed, unmoving. But I'm not thinking about Megan or Harrison. I play the scene in the temple over and over in my mind, letting the feeling of it wash over me. Was it an exhibit of some kind? A trip Dad and I took?

Tonight I need to talk to Dad, to keep my promise to Stephen and to tell him that I remember the temple. For now, I will go downstairs and act normal. When I put my phone on my desk, something long and brown in the pencil holder catches my eye. I grab it and laugh out loud: it's the fudge-bar stick, with Tarin's phone number on it.

I fiddle with the stick a minute, considering options. The old Jessie probably wouldn't have liked Tarin, would have thought she was weird. But maybe the fresh air has gotten to my head, and I'm riding some kind of high from the temple memory and taking those photos. Because I don't give a crap what the Girl would think.

I pick up my phone and punch in Tarin's number.

# Throw Me
# a Line

D ad goes over to his friend's house after dinner to
help again with the calves, and I can't keep my eyes
open long enough to stay up for him. I need to keep my
promise to Stephen, but now it's morning, Dad is sleeping
in, and Mother is taking me to my play date with Tarin.

We've only driven a few minutes down the gravel road,
clouds of dust billowing behind us, when Mother slows
down and signals even though there's no other car in sight.
We turn into a bumpy driveway and there, on the edge of
what isn't exactly a yard but more of a field, is a tiny white
house. There are a few sheds, the paint mostly peeled off,
and a small dirt patch that must be a garden in the making.

When I'd called Tarin, she said, "It's about time! Get
your butt over here already."

"We probably could have walked here," Mother says.
"It's less than a mile. But I've got that soup on the stove
to get back to."

She's waiting, hands tight on the steering wheel, and it hits me: she wants me to go in. Alone. I look at that little place and suddenly my breakfast isn't sitting so well in my stomach. What do I have in common with this girl other than a few random moments spent in a hospital lounge?

Mother reads my mind and opens her door. "Well, I guess I could go say a quick hello to Mrs. Meyer, if she's up for it." When I don't move, she comes around to my side and peers at me through the window. I try to make her proud. I get out and walk beside her up the rickety steps to the front porch, where a fat calico cat looks at us lazily.

Mother knocks on the screen door, and a few seconds later it pops open. A large lady with a gray braid that nearly reaches her waist smiles and waves us in.

"Come in, come in," she says. There's no real entrance— we're standing right in the kitchen, and it smells like cooked cabbage. She introduces herself as Gloria, who I guess must be Tarin's mother, but I don't see any resemblance at all. This woman is more hippie than vampire. Gloria explains that her mother is taking a nap, but invites my mother in for tea. Tarin is downstairs, she says, waiting for me.

I open the door to the basement and walk down the stairs slowly, peering into the semi-darkness, but there's no sign of life. When Tarin appears out of nowhere at the bottom of the stairs, I lose my balance a little and grip the railing to keep from falling. I truly am an overly dramatic freak, and it's embarrassing.

"Welcome to my dungeon," she says. I make it to the last step and follow her around the staircase wall, trying to seem casual as I glance around. A bed, a dresser and a desk barely fit into the space, and a colorful woven rug covers the concrete floor. The walls are concrete too, but a few posters of seventies-style pop art liven things up. Two huge bright-orange cushions lie on the floor. Not too bad for a dungeon, actually.

"Want something to drink?"

I nod and Tarin pulls back a batik wall hanging beside the dresser to reveal a mini kitchen: bar fridge, wooden shelves with mugs and saucers, and even a hot plate sitting on a milk crate.

"This used to be my uncle's bachelor pad," she explains as she takes a can of soda out of the fridge. "I've added the feminine touch, of course. But I've got all the conveniences of home right here, even a small bathroom on the other side of the staircase. Barely need to go upstairs if I don't feel like it. And I usually don't."

"So you mostly hang out down here?"

"Except when I go for walks, yeah. My mom knows by now not to try and force me to do all that fake family-bonding stuff. We got over that a long time ago, when she married my stepdad."

"Oh," I say.

"He's a butthead," she explains. "To put it lightly."

"When do you see your boyfriend?" I ask.

"He lives on the coast," she says. "It's a long-distance thing."

I glance around again. "Do you get bored down here?"

She shrugs. "Not really. I like being on my own, thinking and reading and whatever. I'm a loner, I guess."

I try to get my head around it. She doesn't go to school, doesn't hang out much with her mother or grandmother. Maybe she's like me—napping and watching old home videos and talking to the dog all day. Is someone else really that pathetic?

"Mostly, I'm relieved that I'm not in school anymore. This way I get to avoid all the lame stuff like prom and cheerleading and yearbook committee." She sticks her fingers down her throat in a fake gag.

"Hmm," I say. Right now I can't imagine liking all that either. But once upon a time, I was in there like a dirty shirt.

She leans a little closer. "You used to hang out with that Megan girl, hey? And her friends?"

I nod. "You know them?"

"Only a little. I've seen them a few times, in town. Gran told me you're tight with them."

"Apparently."

"No offense," she says, "but I can't picture it. They seem so sugar-coated."

I shrug. "Maybe I was the rebel of the group."

Her eyes narrow. "Sure."

This would be my chance to bash them, to tell her that they're phonies, especially Megan. But some of the Girl's loyalty must linger inside me, because I don't. "So are you staying here for the rest of the summer?" I ask.

"Don't know. Mom changes her mind every thirty seconds about whether Gran is ready to take care of herself again. We'd take Gran back with us, but she's dead set on staying here in the middle of nowhere. God knows why. No offense."

"None taken." I sip my drink, wondering if Mother is still upstairs or if she's taken off to tend to her soup.

The room is quiet, and Tarin gazes at me with her dark eyes. I brace myself for some kind of deep question, but instead she asks, "Want me to read your palm?"

I'm taken aback for a second, but then I laugh. "You mean, like tell me what all those lines mean and stuff? You can do that?"

"Kind of. I read a book about it when I was a kid, and I've been practicing on all willing victims since. It's sometimes amazingly accurate. I can also read auras." She moves closer to me, picks up my hand and flips it over. I flinch when she runs her finger down the line at the top of my palm.

She pauses. "This okay? It won't hurt or anything."

My whole body is tense, so I take a deep breath and nod. "Knock yourself out."

She examines my hand, running her finger down all the lines. She mutters "hmmm" and "interesting," then finally clears her throat and looks me in the eye.

"This is amazing, actually. Your life line is split in two." She holds my hand up higher. "See?" She points to the line that starts halfway between my thumb and index finger and curves down to the bottom of my palm. It's true—the line begins solid and deep, then breaks off into two sections about one third of the way down.

"What does that mean?"

"Well, I'm only interpreting it, of course. But you've had a major change in your life, with the coma and everything. You're starting again, in a way. So your life line now has branched off, a sort of split between your old self and new self."

It does make sense, I guess. But all I want is for her to tell me that somewhere past the edge of my palm, in a place we can't see, the lines will rejoin and become more solid than ever.

My face must look way too serious, because she looks back at my hand and laughs. "But hey, what do I know? It also says you're going to have seven kids!"

I force myself to smile, but pull my hand away and fold it tightly with the other one in my lap.

"Think my mother is still here?"

"I'm sorry," she says. "That was dumb."

"No," I say. "It was interesting, actually. I'm just a little off today."

"No worries," she says. "Next time we'll do something more exciting. I'll take you to my secret hideout. If you promise not to tell anyone about it, of course."

"Cool," I say. She is an interesting person, and I should try not to be so stiff around her. We make chitchat about stuff like TV shows and how lame Katy Perry is, and then Mother calls down the stairs that she should head home before the soup explodes, but I'm welcome to stay.

"I'm coming too," I yell back. There are polite good-byes at the door, and Tarin tells me not to be a stranger.

"I didn't mean to rush you," Mother says when we're in the car. "Did it go all right?"

I nod, because I guess it did.

Mother clears her throat. "Gloria told me Tarin takes courses online. Maybe you should try that for a while, until you're ready to go back to school."

"All right," I say. I'm surprised that Mother would even think out of the box like that, and relieved that she's not pushing the school thing on me. But even though I know I'm being a loser, the only thing I care about right now is what Tarin told me. About my split life line.

First I have an abnormal brain. And now this?

# Illusions

Finally, the window of opportunity I've been waiting for. Mother takes a bubble bath, then gives me a goodnight peck on the cheek; Stephen is upstairs in his room, pouting. So Dad and I are alone in the living room, and it's my chance to keep my word to Stephen and convince Dad that we need to stay on the farm.

Dad flicks through the channels, yawning and munching on a bowl of nuts. He finally settles on a nature show with huge blubbering walruses stabbing at each other with their tusks, bright blood clouding the water. It's disturbing, and it's making it hard for me to get into the right frame of mind for a heart-to-heart. Plus, I don't really have a plan.

"Dad?" I finally say, when the scene switches to penguins.

He turns down the volume a little, thankfully, because the penguin honking is crazy loud. "Yeah?" When he faces me, I see the weariness in his eyes. A brain-damaged daughter, a son who's mad at him, a crying wife, giving up his farm, pulling out baby calves two nights in a row—it's a lot for one guy to take.

I shouldn't be nervous, I know. But what if I can't make him understand how much Stephen is counting on me to turn things around? And the way he looks at me, so worn out by it all, I can't do it. Not yet. "I remembered something," I say.

He turns the penguins down even more and leans closer. "What is it?"

My hands clench together. "The temple." He is still waiting, his eyebrows raised. "I remember visiting the temple with you."

He leans back again, and it's clear from his expression that he's not getting what I'm talking about. But he couldn't have forgotten something so magical.

"You know, the Temple of Dendur. From Egypt. We saw it together." I don't mean it to, but my voice comes out sounding annoyed. "It was big, and beautiful, and amazing."

His eyebrows wrinkle up. "Right," he says. "Right, that."

"Yeah, that," I say. I thought his face would light up, but there isn't a trace of joy in his eyes. "Aren't you happy I remember?"

Dad lets out a long sigh, closing his eyes tight. I wait patiently while he gathers himself. His eyes pop back open. He reaches out and puts an arm around my shoulder.

"My dear Jess," he says. "We never went to the Temple of Dendur."

My chest tightens. "Yes," I say. "Yes, we did. I remember it clearly, like it was yesterday." I shrug his arm off my shoulder.

"Jess." He looks straight into my eyes. "That was not us. That was Megan and her dad. They went to see it, in New York. We were supposed to go with them, but you ended up in the hospital."

Even though I don't think he would lie to me—why would he?—I can't believe it. The memory of that place with its tall columns, and the echo of Dad's voice, felt so real. "No." I shake my head. "No. It's not true."

Dad doesn't try to convince me. He puts his arm around me again, and this time I let him. A sob carries through me, so sudden and sharp that I cry out. I lean into him, my face on his chest, and let the wave of disappointment pass through me.

"I don't get it," I wail. "It seemed so real."

He rubs my back, mutters that it's all right, that it doesn't matter. But we both know it's a big deal: my mind is playing tricks on me.

When I am spent, a small shudder passes though me, and I sit up. "I promised Stephen," I say, "that I would convince you not to sell the farm."

"And what about you?" he says. "Do you want to stay?"

I gaze up at him, at those soft eyes, and I know that maybe if I say yes, it could change something. If I could only tell him that this farm means everything to me too, that I cherish the woods and the bison and the times we spent here together. I did enjoy taking photos outside, did feel the beginnings of a connection to this place. But I'm not sure that's enough. I can't tell him what I want when it's obvious that I can't even trust my own mind. I am too worn out to lie.

"I don't know," I say.

# A Walk on the Wild Side

Another Thursday, another visit to the friendly neighborhood shrink. Dr. K. asks to see my homework, then praises my efforts on the letter to the Girl. She asks how my week was.

I sit there in that uncomfortable chair and rattle off a list of what went wrong: the love of my ex-life thinks I'm faking amnesia, my best friend defended him, and my parents put our farm up for sale. I tell her about my temple memory too, and how my mind deceived me. And how I couldn't bring myself to convince Dad not to sell the farm, and how this morning when I told Stephen that I had failed, he didn't get mad or anything. All he did was sigh and go back to hiding out in his room.

I've never seen such a stunned look on the doctor's beautiful face.

We spend the rest of the hour talking about each of these events, and Dr. K. asks me to describe my feelings:

mad, hurt, embarrassed, worried, disappointed, guilty. I think I name every emotion known to humankind. My heart feels heavy and tired, but I don't break down or freak out or anything. I feel cold, oddly detached, like I am talking about someone else's life. On some level, I guess I am.

When our time is almost up, Dr. K. explains my new homework assignment. "I know you don't remember your recent years, what your life was like. But let's not worry about that for now. I want you to write a few pages about what you would like your life to be like now, in the present. What things you want to do, what people you want to spend time with. How about you call it My Perfect Life?"

Sounds futile to me to wish for what you can't have. But I nod obediently, and she stands up to give me a hug.

Last time we came to the city, I fell asleep before we could go to Taco Time, apparently my old favorite. When Mother asks if I'd like to finally go there for lunch, I don't have the heart to say no. She's jumpy, knocking her coffee over so it spills all over my burrito. Maybe she wants to talk about the farm thing, but she doesn't bring it up. I'm guessing Dad told her about my false memory too, but she doesn't mention that either. When we pull up in the driveway at home, I'm so relieved that I pop the door open before Mother has even gotten the key out of the ignition.

I bound up the sidewalk and nearly trip on a rusty old bike. Tarin sits on our steps, munching on a bag of chips.

"Hey," she says. "Hope you don't mind me turning up like this."

I don't have time to answer; Mother is right behind me. "Well," she says, "hello there."

Tarin doesn't pick up on the what-the-hell-are-you-doing-here vibe. She stands up and leans on my shoulder. "Mrs. Grenier, can I borrow Jessica? I'll have her back in an hour or so. Going for a little nature walk." Mother looks unsure, but Tarin hooks arms with me and leads me away from the door.

"Thanks!" Tarin says.

Mother pauses, watching us, then nods slowly before she disappears into the house.

"Wow," I say. "You have a way with mothers."

"You've got to be confident," she explains, "but respectful. Works like a charm."

She pulls me toward the garage, glancing around like she's looking for something. "Which way to the cut line?" she says. "I know how to get to my secret hideaway from there."

"Is that where you're taking me? Is this kidnapping or something?"

"Sure," she says. "You could call it that."

I laugh, and I'm glad that she's here to take my mind off—well, everything.

"So? You know where it is?" she asks, the sun reflecting off her nose rings.

When I'd visited the bison, I had seen a long clearing that ran past their pen. "Maybe."

"The blind leading the blind. Now this should be an adventure." She looks around again, and her eyes land on the For Sale sign. "Whoa. What the hell?"

"I'll tell you about it as we walk," I say, and I lead her this time, behind the house and on to where the clearing is. I tell her about Stephen and how upset he is, and how I can't decide how I feel. How even Dad seems confused.

"Yikes," she says. "A real-life soap opera."

I almost tell her about the fake memory, but she starts going on about her stepfather and how he controls her mom, and how it disgusts her that her mother has no spine. If it weren't for her boyfriend and music and knowing one day she'll be old enough to be on her own, she says, she'd completely lose it.

When we get to the clearing, she nods. "This must be it. It should lead us to the creek, and then I'll know how to get there." We make our way down the cut line, bees buzzing around our heads and grasshoppers leaping in the tall grass. Tarin and I get into a rhythm, taking our steps in unison, and it feels good to be moving, not thinking.

The cut line opens into a wider space, a field with trees sprinkled through it. We pick up the pace and stride across the clearing, then come to a small creek winding its way around the trees.

"Bingo!" Tarin exclaims. The creek is shallow enough that we could probably walk across it.

Tarin shields her eyes from the sun with her hand and looks slowly from one side of the bank to the other. "There's an old log bridge that I cross when I go from my place, so it must be on your side of the creek. And that way"—she points to the left, where a clump of tall pine trees stands—"should be north." She turns to me suddenly. "I've never taken anyone there, you know."

"I'm honored to be the chosen one," I say. "Now get your butt in gear and find it already."

We tramp along the side of the creek, Tarin occasion-ally stopping to study her surroundings, and then she turns and heads into the trees. A small path leads through the bush, and by the way she pulls me in there, I guess we are getting warmer.

"This is it!" Only a few minutes' walk, feet crunching leaves and snapping twigs, and the trees give way to a small clearing.

"Ta-da!" she says with a sweep of her arms. "Not exactly the Taj Mahal, but it's all I've got." A rusty old camper, the kind that sits on the back of a truck, is propped up on cement blocks. It looks like the smallest breeze would send it toppling onto its side.

I can't pinpoint what I expected, exactly, but this piece of junk doesn't look like much, abandoned and with tall weeds growing up around it.

"Who does it belong to?" I ask.

"I have no idea. I've been coming here since we moved to Gran's a few months ago, and I've never seen any sign of life or anything."

"What do you do out here?"

She takes a swipe at the grass with her stick. "Hang out. Read. Write in my journal. Get away from my mom."

Obviously, she needs to get things off her chest. But why would I want to deal with someone else's issues when I can't even handle my own? Tarin drops the stick, steps closer and whispers, although there's no one to hear but the birds and squirrels. "I've even spent the night here a few times."

"By yourself?" I ask.

"No, with a male stripper."

I laugh. "Can I have a tour?"

"Absolutely, darling." Planting her feet firmly on the ground, she grabs the door handle and yanks it hard. It pops open, and she takes a step up to climb into the dark cave of the camper. I follow her and am hit with a disgusting smell that makes me gag.

"God, what died in here?"

"It's not that bad. You'll get used to it. Now let me open up the curtains a little." A soft light fills the room. There's a table with benches on either side. The benches are covered in hideous green upholstery spotted with holes, and by the door is a two-burner stove.

"Where do you sleep?" I ask.

She sits on one of the benches and leans on the table. I'm not getting used to the smell. "Up there." She points to an area above the table, where there's a camouflage sleeping bag lying on a dingy foam mattress. She observes me for a few seconds like she wants me to say something, maybe "how cozy" or "this is awesome," but no polite blah-blah comes out of my mouth. She gives up and gestures for me to sit down.

"Make yourself at home." The table is smeared with something red.

"It's only ketchup," she says, reading my mind. "I made a fire and roasted a hot dog last time, and I didn't have anything to wipe up the mess." She gazes around, her face softening with affection. "I love this little getaway. Sometimes I can't take my life for another millisecond."

She is my new friend, and I should be more supportive, but all I can think is: Shit, here it comes.

"I know your problems are bigger than mine," she says, "but really, Mom and I can't stand each other anymore. I can't stand her for marrying Fraser, and she can't stand me at all. At least here, out in the boonies, I can get away from her a little. When Gran's better and we go back home to our tiny apartment with Mr. Jerkface, there's nowhere to hide. I don't think I can do it again."

I nod and try not to look at the ketchup smears, because they are really bothering me. "That sucks" are the only words of wisdom I can come up with.

"Can you keep a secret?" she asks.

I don't know if I want to know the secret, exactly, but I know that keeping it to myself will not be a problem. I don't have any real friends to tell. I nod.

"I have a plan," she says. "To take off. For good."

"What?" I say. "Like running away?"

She nods, a flash of determination in her eyes. "Yeah. I'm going to get away from all that crap. Take off and start over. I've been thinking about it for ages, but I think I'm finally ready."

"Wow," I say. "Where will you go?"

"I'll come here first for a few days, then wherever. Doesn't matter. As long as no one knows me and I never have to see my stepdad again." She sits up straight and locks me into one of those searing stares of hers.

"I'll send you a signal, when I finally do it. You could come with me."

"I'll think about it," I say, and suddenly the weight of this whole scene—the depressing camper, her desperation to get away—is too much. My fragile psyche is not in any condition to handle more strife; it's reached its maximum quota for the next few decades at least.

I stand up. "I need to get back," I say. "My mother's probably worried."

Tarin frowns, and I think maybe she's going to make some smart-ass comment about me being a goody-goody, but instead she gets up too. "Sorry to lay that on you. I guess"—she sighs—"I guess I trust you."

I wish I could say the same, but I'm hesitant. I don't even trust myself these days. She clears her throat and pushes the door open. "Let's get you back home."

We walk in silence until we reach my front door. I ask her if she wants to come in for a cookie or something, but she shakes her head. "Homework to do."

She's already on her bike in the driveway when dread suddenly washes over me. She may be complicated, but she's the only friend I've got. I call after her, "Hey, Tarin!"

She pauses, waiting for me to speak.

"Ever been to a pit party?"

She wrinkles her brow for a second, then lets out a loud laugh. "No, but it's been a lifelong dream."

# Enchanted Forest

I spend the afternoon before the pit party reading the rest of the flowered journal from the shoebox. There are only about ten entries after the eulogy: the Girl writes about her dreams for the future (true love, big house, blah, blah, blah), the politics on a school dance committee, and her fights with Mother. Nothing earth-shattering. But the last entry, from early April, gets my attention.

*Today at school, I wanted to die. Megan was going around making a list of Most Likely suggestions for the yearbook. Most Likely to End Up in Prison, Most Likely to Marry a Billionaire, that kind of stuff. They were all funny, and we were all laughing. But then, when it came to me, Harrison said: Most Likely to Be Wearing Old-Lady Underwear. The whole room cracked up. I laughed too, but then I had to hide in a bathroom stall and cry during Chemistry. I told Megan I was having an allergic reaction to someone's perfume.*

*Maybe she knew the truth, but she didn't push it. It was humiliating. The worst part is, he's right. I am boring. I hate being boring. I hate being myself. Maybe one day I'll work up the guts to do something crazy, to show everyone that there's more to me than meets the eye. But I'm not even sure there is.*

I read it again, letting it sink in. So the Girl knew she was boring, and it bothered her. And then my mind goes even further, makes a leap I have no way of testing: maybe the Girl was so miserable in this mundane little life of hers that it pushed her to do something totally off the deep end. Like climbing into a bison pen. Maybe, as much as I don't want to consider it, the Girl had a death wish.

These are heavy thoughts, and I push them to the back of my mind. I have to deal with something more pressing: choosing my outfit for my first pit party. I end up going with jeans and a nice black sweater.

Deceiving my mother is the next step, and it's surprisingly easy. She would probably let me go if I said I was going to a party with Megan and the Pink Posse. But Tarin? It's easier to tell her that Tarin has invited me over to watch a few movies. Only Tarin's mom is going to be out at bingo, and Tarin has convinced her granny to let her use her Oldsmobile. Never mind that Tarin only has her learner's license—there are no cops for miles around, and the route to the party is on side roads.

When Mother drops me off, Tarin is decked out in a long black dress with an oversized leather jacket and wears dark-purple lipstick. Not my look exactly—don't know what that is yet–but somehow she pulls it off.

"Let's rock and roll." Keys dangle at the end of her fingertips. "Thanks, Gran," she calls to the living room. "Don't wait up. We're going for ice cream and might stop in at Jessica's friend's place."

A soft "Okay, dear" carries over the sound of the TV, and we head out to the car. It's huge and dusty, and when I slide into the passenger side I come face to face with a Hello Kitty air freshener hanging from the rearview mirror. The cord is wrapped around her neck.

"Had to jazz the ride up a little," Tarin says. It takes a few turns of the key for the car to rumble to a start, and then we are barreling down the dusty road, and panic builds in my chest. What's Megan going to say when she sees me? Did I think I could simply slip in unnoticed?

Tarin clicks on the radio, and loud static blasts out. She pushes buttons until a voice sings, *I'm radioactive, radioactive!*

"You all right?" Tarin asks. "You're as white as a virgin on her wedding night."

I nod. "I think so."

She glances at me as she slides past a yield sign. "All you need is an adventure to put some color in your cheeks," she says. "Have no fear, Tarin is here."

I laugh and crank the music up louder, and we sing along at the top of our lungs. "*Welcome to the new age, to the new age!*"

The pit is about a twenty-minute drive away, past a little homemade-looking golf course. The field next to the pit is full of cars and pickups. Tarin parks beside an old green truck and shuts off the car.

Someone's made a bonfire, and there's a card table set up with speakers on it. Clusters of kids stand around in circles. It's nuts that I'm even here.

"Come on," Tarin says, shaking my shoulder. "Let's rock this thing." We open our doors and step out, and I swear I can feel my heart pounding in my ears.

"Jessie?" A voice comes from behind, and when I turn I am face to face with Megan. She looks shocked, like someone has slapped her in the face.

The plan comes to me suddenly. "Surprise!" I say weakly. "I was going to call you but thought it'd be more fun to just show up."

"Okay," she says. She's not buying it, but she smiles politely anyway. She glances toward Tarin, who is sitting on the hood of the car. Tarin cracks her knuckles, and I see her through Megan's eyes: she's crude, weird, even a bit freaky.

"This is Tarin," I say. "My neighbor. She said I could catch a ride."

Tarin's eyes narrow, but she doesn't rat me out. "Hey," she says.

Megan smiles, but it's not her usual megawatt grin. "Nice to meet you." She stands there looking at me, and I have to remind myself that she's the one who let me down, defending that shithead Harrison.

"Gotta go check my lip gloss," I say. "Meet you over there." Megan nods and walks off.

"Man," Tarin says, "we've got to get you out of her spell. Before you turn all princessy too."

I start to defend Megan. "Hey, she's—" but before I can even finish, Tarin has shoved a cold bottle into my hand. I hold it up, read the label.

"Beer?" I say. "Where'd you get this? And is this a good idea?"

She shrugs it off. "My uncle leaves a stash under the stairs in the basement, to make his visits more tolerable. And I can tell from your questions that you know even less than I do about pit parties. Why do you think it's out here in the middle of nowhere? Do you think everyone came out here to play leapfrog?" She twists the cap off her beer and it lets out a hiss, and then she chugs back half of the bottle in one long swig.

She wipes her mouth and burps. "Go on. Trust me, it's the only way you'll get through this."

I lift the bottle to my mouth. The beer is cold and bitter, but I do what Tarin did—I chug down half of it.

"See?" she says. "That wasn't so hard."

I feel fine, so I do the same with the rest of the bottle, and so does Tarin. Then she grabs my arm and we walk around the cars and over to the action. Loud music blasts out of the speakers. Megan and the Posse are talking to some guys and don't notice me walk up, but a few random people glance over my way. This is all right, I tell myself. I can be normal.

More people arrive with cases of beer. Tarin and I stand to the side, watching the scene. I'm a little light-headed, but it's a nice feeling, so I go back with Tarin to the car and chug another beer.

A few girls come up to me and say hello, and some even fill me in on how we used to know each other: yearbook committee, French class, Girl Guides. I'm a little embarrassed that I don't remember them, but I find myself making jokes—and they laugh. I feel looser, more relaxed, than I can remember ever feeling. I think I might actually be having fun.

Tarin goes to the car while I am chatting and brings me another beer. I'm already floating, my feet barely touching the sandy earth, so I sip that one. Warmth travels from my head to the tips of my toes.

"Whoa," she says. "Your aura is amazing right now. Green, pink, purple, all swirling together."

I laugh. "And you, in case I've never told you, are one cool chick!"

We high-five each other, and then Tarin points to a short guy wearing a tuque over his long hair. "I know that dude," she says. "Be right back."

"Hey." A voice comes from behind, and when I turn around, Harrison is standing there, smiling at me. Heat rises in my cheeks.

"Hey to you," I say. We look at each other, and those damn dimples of his make it hard for me to slap him.

"Didn't see you at school again," he says.

"Nope," I answer. And when I look at him and that cocky smile, I know he thinks I have a thing for him. Who knows how many years I followed him around, drooling over him, feeding his ego?

I can't tell if it's the beer or if I'm truly not mad anymore, but I suddenly don't like him or hate him. I don't even care. My head is buzzing a little. "See you around," I say. He looks surprised as I push past him and make my way toward Megan and her circle.

"Jessie!" Kerry yells. "Finally coming to say hi to your old gang." She hooks arms with me and winks. Megan is watching me closely, and I know she knows I am tipsy.

I nod and smile, smile and nod.

"You okay?" she asks.

Nod and smile. "Smurfy." My bladder is suddenly on the verge of exploding. "Where's the ladies' room?"

Cybil points to the trees on the edge of the pit. "I'll come with you," she says, but I wave her off.

"Thanks, Mom. I can handle it."

I imagine I am in rehab again and concentrate on taking straight, careful steps toward the bushes. Once there I find a spot behind a big spruce and lower my pants. Instant relief. I zip up, straighten out my sweater and lean against a tree. Taking deep breaths, I mentally prepare myself for acting "normal," then walk toward the edge of the woods to make my way back.

"Well, hello."

The voice comes from my left, ground level. Sitting cross-legged in the leaves, back against a tree trunk, is a guy with strawberry-blond hair and a red-and-black-checkered lumberjack shirt. "Where'd you come from? You some kind of forest pixie or something?" he says.

"Yeah, and you must be an ogre?"

His chuckle is low and soft. "You wouldn't be the first to call me that."

Without even thinking about it, I plunk myself down right beside him. We sit in silence for a few minutes, and I have to close my eyes to stop the spinning in my head.

"What's your name?" he asks.

I look at him through barely open eyelids, trying to gauge if he's only keeping up the game. Everyone in Winding Creek knows everyone. Except the one, me, who has forgotten everyone else, that is. He's not smiling. "Jessie," I answer. "Do we know each other?"

"Don't think I've had the pleasure, Jessie. I'm Dan. Jeffrey Hill's cousin. Just here for the weekend."

"Okay," I say. My mouth feels dry and chalky, and I see he's got a Coke bottle beside him. I know I'm totally winning him over with my wit and charm so far, so I reach for it and take a swig. It's not plain Coke—it burns like fire going down—but somehow I don't choke.

He laughs that soft chuckle again. "Whoa," he says. "I'd take it easy on that. Jeff mixed it up for me, said he wanted to put hair on my chest. I was going to dump it out here in the woods."

"Sorry," I say. "I got thirsty all of a sudden."

"No apology necessary," he says. "*Me casa es su casa.*"

Whatever was in that bottle is making the fuzziness of the beer turn to a feeling of peace and love and harmony. I take another swig, then another.

"You sure you want to do that, little pixie?" he says. "It's not Kool-Aid." But the way he says it is gentle and teasing, and when I lean closer I see that he has total puppy-dog eyes.

"What are you doing out here, away from the action?" I ask. My words feel slippery and loose, but I can't tell if that's only in my mind.

"Beats me, really," he answers. "I guess I'm not in the mood for all the blah-blah yada yada. Maybe I'm weird."

"No, no," I say and find myself falling closer toward him. "Sounds normal to me. It's serene, hanging out with the trees."

"For sure," he says. "You guys don't know how good you have it, living here. You can step out into the wild anytime you like."

His voice is soothing. My head spins, and I have to reach out and prop my arm on the ground to keep from toppling over.

"You all right?" he asks. I tilt my head, and it's crazy, because the only thoughts I've had about kissing a guy were to wonder if I ever had, but my body wants to touch him in some way, and the mouth seems the most logical. I hone in on him in what feels like slow motion. He's looking at me with this odd expression, like he's not sure if he should or not but maybe wants to, when suddenly my stomach lurches.

I struggle to my feet, but my head is heavy and I stumble. The ogre leaps up to steady me. His arms go around my shoulders, and this overwhelming feeling of being alive washes over me. Tears start to pool in my eyes. Ramses did not kill me. I am here now, and it's beautiful. My shoulders heave as I sob and fall to my knees. Then I lean forward and empty the contents of my stomach into the leaves. Dan holds me and mutters kind words like, "No big deal, little pixie. It's all right. You'll be fine."

Suddenly Megan is there, and Kerry, and they are going on and on about looking for me everywhere and where the hell is that friend of mine with the nose rings. Then Tarin is there too, announcing loudly that everyone should take a chill pill, that everything is under control. The next thing I know, I am in the back of a car, stretched out across the seat, my eyes heavy.

Farewell, handsome ogre.

# Pièce de Résistance

My head pounds, and I feel like I've eaten a bag of sawdust. Mother knocks on my door and peers in my room. "You do look rough. Tarin told me about the bad sushi," she says. "I canceled your appointment with Dr. K. Do you think we should take you to the doctor?"

I shake my head. "I'm fine." When she's gone, I pop some aspirin. Bad sushi. I'm not surprised that smooth Tarin would come up with some creative explanation to save my butt. I sleep most of the day away, and when I finally drag myself downstairs I find only Stephen in the living room. A soccer game plays on TV, but there's no sound.

"Mom and Dad are in town," he says stiffly. "With the agent. There's been an offer on the farm." I sit beside him, wishing I could help, wishing I could use some positive thinking to make everything better. Instead, I choke down some dry cereal, say goodnight and head back to my room.

What's a girl with brain damage supposed to do anyway?

I wake up in the middle of the night, headache gone. I toss and turn and think about how my life is about to change. I don't know if Mother and Dad accepted the offer, or what's going to happen now. I head downstairs and sit in the half darkness of the basement, watching the news channel. In the world there are:

Starving children with ribs that stick out.

People living in refugee camps, with little food and no home to go back to.

Children who have been kidnapped.

Children who have been drowned in the bathtub by their own mothers.

Tsunamis and earthquakes and tornadoes and hurricanes that rip up towns like they are made of Tinkertoys.

Drive-by shootings and rapes and serial killings.

Kids with bombs strapped onto their stomachs who get on buses and blow themselves up.

And then, here at home on our cozy couch with a bowl of cereal in her lap, there's me.

Poor me, poor me. I'm hung over and I made a fool of myself. I don't remember everything about my picture-perfect, spoiled existence with loving parents and a nice house and enough food to make me obese. Poor me, my parents want to sell the farm that I don't even know if I like. One of my memories wasn't real at all, and my brother is disappointed in me. Cry me a river.

Dr. K. is trying to teach me to be grateful for what I have, but I am failing miserably. I can't shake this feeling of self-pity. Who is Jessica Grenier, in the big scheme of things? I am a drop in the bucket, and my problems aren't even a grain of sand in the Sahara.

I need to get over myself.

I march upstairs and grab my cell phone. I could sneak outside and take some moonlit photos, but the mere thought of the effort required wears me out. I go back to the basement instead and turn on Mother's laptop. While it's booting up, I go through the photos I took outside— the picnic table, Ginger, the trees, the sky—and email them to myself.

A few minutes later I have the pictures open in the photo-editing program.

I click on a shot of Ginger, looking up at me with her soulful eyes.

"Aw, look at you," I say. It's a nice pic, with a tenderness to it, but it lacks a certain something. I find the Edit button and move the slider to make the photo dark, then overly bright. I do the same with the contrast. I try Ginger in sepia and in black-and-white. It's strangely soothing to see her morph and change at my fingertips, so I go back to my files and try the same with the photo of the picnic table. I want to do something more, something crazier. I click around the menus until I find Editing Options.

I start with the Ginger shot, cropping and cutting and changing colors. Then I open a few other photos in new windows: the picnic table, a shot of some clouds floating lonely in the sky, another of the squirrel. I play with them one by one until they all look funky and wild and a little surreal. So much better than they were before. A button at the top says *Layers*, so I open all the new images and drag and drop the photos until I've created a full-screen image of the four shots melded into one.

Ginger, a bright red, in the top left corner; the squirrel, striped like a zebra, on the right. In the lower left corner, the picnic table; beside it, the single cloud, a soft pink, floating in pale-blue sky. It's a crazy patchwork collage. Probably something a kindergartener could do, I know. But it feels good looking at what I have made. The images and colors speak to me; they stir something up inside. It's especially the cloud, that drifting bit of pink fluff, that draws me in, and the reason comes to me slowly.

That lone cloud is me. Floating, distant, watching everyone from above. Untouchable. I save the collage with the name *Twisted Nature*, then click *Print*, and it comes out of the printer. I'm shutting down the computer when a text appears on my phone.

It's from Tarin. All it says is Taj Mahal. Tonight.

# A Fine Kettle
of Fish

I'm going out of my mind. Mother and Dad are going back and forth, negotiating offers with the people who want the farm, and I brace myself for a call from Tarin's mother. I can't believe Tarin's out there by herself at the camper, and I know I should tell someone. But how can I betray her? She may be messed up, but she is the one person who doesn't mind that I am too.

But her mother doesn't call all day and not that night either. The next morning I get up and pace—I can't stand the waiting. I need to do something, anything, to stop thinking about Tarin.

Stephen is sitting at his desk, reading a book on volcanoes. "Bro," I say, peering down over his shoulder, "we need to blow off some steam. Let's do something wacky."

He shakes his head. "I've got homework."

I don't blame him for not wanting to hang out with me. But I think he needs shaking out of a funk too.

"Please, brother of mine?" I beg. "I promise we'll have fun. I even have a great idea."

My fingers find the top of his head and tousle his hair. Swinging around in the chair, he reaches up and clamps his fingers tight around my arm. "What am I," he says, irritated, "your pet monkey?"

I could sit there all day, feeling the warmth of those fingers, but if I let it go on even a second longer, I risk creeping him out. "Yeah!" I yell, wrestling my way out of his clutches. "Dance, my little pet!"

We lunge back and forth at each other until he whacks me so hard in the knee that I fall to the floor. He collapses beside me and actually laughs for the first time in days.

"You're such a moron," he says.

"Takes one to know one."

We gaze up at the ceiling.

"What's the plan then?" Stephen says. "Did you tear me away from my scientific studies just to be annoying?"

"Sorry, Einstein." I search my mental list of activities for something a ten-year-old might like, but the best I come up with is "How about we go fishing?"

He wrinkles his nose. "What? That's lame."

For once, my on-the-fritz brain does some quick thinking. "Did I mention that it's spearfishing?"

Now I've got his attention. His eyes widen, but then he shakes his head. "Do you think Mom and Dad would let us do that?"

"Dad?" I say. "You saw that giant stuffed fish in the basement. He'd be proud of our initiative."

But he doesn't look convinced, so I pull out the big guns. "It might be our last chance to do this kind of stuff," I say. "Do you think we'll have a creek behind our house if we move to town? We'll be fishing in the bathtub."

I don't feel good about it exactly, but it works. He puts down his pencil and we're on our way outside.

———

It's a scene straight out of a hillbilly movie: Stephen in Dad's ratty old straw hat and rubber boots halfway up his thighs, me in humongous hip waders, carrying the "spears" we made by tying kitchen knives to the ends of broomsticks after unscrewing the broom heads. I can practically hear the banjo playing in the background.

I want to take the quad to the creek, but Stephen is worried someone will hear the noise. I assure him that the giant fans Mother has on all over the house will block the sound, and I must be right, because no one comes running when he reluctantly fires up the quad. I hang on the back with the spears pointing upward as he drives down the cut line. When we get to the creek, he shuts the machine off and we peer down at the water. The water isn't much deeper than it was when I came with Tarin, and I have no idea if there are even fish in there. It's weird being there, so close to the camper where

Tarin must be right now. And I can't even tell Stephen about it.

"So what now?" he says. "We throw these things into the water at the fish? That's it?"

"I guess," I answer, and I begin my descent down the bank. "C'mon, Earl. If we's gonna fry us up a tasty supper tonight, we's best get fishin'."

We both slide, slightly off-balance, until we are on a narrow, grassy bank slightly above the creek. Stephen pulls the straw hat back up from his forehead. "Is there enough water in there to hold any fish?"

The creek does look a little lifeless, but I maintain my enthusiasm. "Of course. Where would they all go? Hitchhike to the ocean?"

Stephen reaches toward me and takes a spear from my grip, a twinkle in his eyes—maybe not of excitement, exactly, but of curiosity at least. "Lead me to them," he says.

We splash our way through the creek, the black rubber of our boots never getting wet past our knees, until we reach what looks like the deepest part. Leaning over, we peer into the murky water. I can't make out any signs of life. Please, fish, I mentally beg, give me this.

Stephen stands up and tentatively jabs his spear at the surface. "How are we going to know they're coming? I can't see a thing."

It's a legitimate question—even a dumb kid would ask that—but I'm not going to let him see that I'm shaking in my waders. I'll find a way to make this work.

"Well, that's part of the challenge. You think the Blackfoot people could see the fish when they did this, not for fun like us, but to keep their families from starvation? In fact, they used to fish at night, because that's when the most fish are out feeding."

He studies the water. "Hmmm." He's probably thinking I'm the biggest liar—and he'd be right—but then he nods slowly. "They were probably a lot more in tune with nature than we are. Could probably sense the presence of the fish or their spirits. Something like that."

"Cool, huh?" I say.

For a few seconds we listen to the gentle gurgling of the water and breathe in the fresh air, pretending what I've told him is true. I take a deep breath, grasp my spear tightly and raise my hands as high as I can above my head. "Ready?"

Stephen does the same. A heartbeat later and— slam!—the blades slice into the shallow water. Pumping our arms up and down, crying out like warriors, we stab at the invisible fish. With each exit from the water, the empty blades reflect sunlight. We thrust madly, over and over, our voices growing bolder and wilder.

I think about Tarin and the farm and Ramses and the Girl I can't be no matter how hard I try. And I let it all flow out of me, off my back and down my fingertips, with each and every stab. It feels crazy good.

Then, as suddenly as we began, Stephen stops stabbing, stops his warrior cries and lets his spear fall into the water. It takes me a few seconds to slow down and stop too.

"Maybe it's not our day," he says. "My vibe tells me there are no fish."

I want to agree with him, let it go and head home, laughing about what idiots we are. But I know there's got to be at least one piddly little fish in that pathetic creek, one sucker that will justify dragging him out here.

So I beg. "Come on, don't give up now. It's only been a few minutes. We've probably picked a bad spot, that's all. Let's try"—I scan the water, searching for a place that looks even the slightest bit more promising—"over there, closer to the bank. It's a little shadier. I bet the fish like that."

He can surely sense the desperation in my voice, because he humors me. "Yeah, maybe. We can try it, I guess." He lifts his spear out of the water and splashes his way toward the opposite shore.

"Here, little fishies!"

The water is murkier in our new spot, so once again we stab blindly at our prey. Nothing. There are no warrior cries this time, only pure concentration. Each and every slash reveals an empty blade, and my shoulders begin to ache. Stephen stops finally, breathing hard from the workout. "Looks like we ain't havin' no supper tonight, Jim Bob," he says.

I hear him but not really, because the pain in my arms feels kind of good. I've never wanted anything so badly, and I keep stabbing, faster and faster. I can feel Stephen's gaze as he watches my movements grow stronger and wilder. It's so simple: the connection with some fish tissue—even the tiniest slice through a tail or a fin—will make me happy. Can't the universe give me at least that?

"Jess," he says softly. "Let's go home."

It only fuels my desire. If I don't catch something soon, right away, he will make me go home. I lunge forward now with each stab, breathing fast and heavy. The broomstick quivers slightly in my hand when the blade shimmies off the occasional rock. *Fish*, I want to scream, *where the hell are you*? My jaw is tight, and every muscle in my body works toward this one stupid goal.

And then…jackpot! The spear has sliced into something, something that is not rock or mud. Something alive. I yelp in triumph, and when I pull the spear up to see my catch, I feel the blade slide out of the tissue. But when it breaks the surface of the water, it is empty.

And then the air is filled with a howl, almost animal-like. Stephen he is doubled over in the water, red swirling at his feet.

The realization nearly gags me: there is no fish.

The flesh at the end of that blade was Stephen.

My fatigued arms find the strength to scoop Little Man up, and, splashing and half-tripping on rocks, I carry him across the creek to the four-wheeler and sit him down. Blood is pouring from a slice in his rubber boot: it's his foot that I hit. He chews on his bottom lip, his hands clutching at his leg.

"Oh my god. Holy shit," I sputter. "Why were you standing so close to me?"

I regret it as soon as it comes out. But Stephen doesn't flinch. "You never listen to me," he croaks. "I wanted you to stop." He slumps forward, his face pasty white.

"I know," I say. "I'm a moron, I know. I'm going to fix this, I promise." My heart pounds so fast I can feel it in my throat. I have to stay calm. I don't think it's a good idea to take off the boot, but even if it were, I don't think I could bring myself to look at what I've done. I grab the bandanna off the straw hat and tie it tightly around his boot, a few inches above the gash. Stephen yelps and reaches down to squeeze my shoulder.

"That'll stop the bleeding, at least until we get home," I say. As gently as I can, I ease his leg over the seat and place it on the footrest. "Hang on to me."

My shaking hands manage to find the key and turn it, and somehow, in spurts and stalls, I figure out how to drive. We make it back down the cut line, Stephen's arms wrapped around me.

I don't bother parking the quad in the shop but instead pull right up to the front door of the house and cut the ignition. My fingers peel Stephen's arms from me, and I turn around.

"How are you doing back there?" My voice sounds like gravel.

He doesn't have a chance to answer. Standing behind the quad, arms calmly at her side, is our mother.

"Cybil's mom called," she says. "She told me you were at a party on Saturday. And you were *drunk*."

Her face is red, like it's taking all she's got not to scream at me. But right now all that matters is Little Man.

"Help me," I say. "Please."

"What's going on?" Mother says.

I look at Stephen in some idiotic hope that he will have an explanation, but he is staring down at the ground.

"He's hurt," I choke out, and then I slide my arm under Stephen's legs, step off the seat and lift him up.

"What do you mean, hurt?" Mother says, her voice high. "What happened?" I am already up the stairs, and Mother opens the door and guides us into the warmth of the living room. *Home*, I think, for the first time I can remember.

Then Dad is there and Stephen is stretched out on the couch. I know he can't be dying or anything—can he?—but he must be in shock or something, because he is really out of it. Dad unties the bandanna, and Mother runs to the bathroom to get the first-aid kit.

"What in God's name happened?" Dad asks me. "How did he get this cut? Did he fall? Where were you?"

I want to answer. But how can I possibly explain that all I wanted to do was stop all the seriousness and worry and have some laughs, and so we decided to go spearfishing? "We were at the creek," I mumble.

Mother is there now, shaking a brown bottle of antiseptic and asking Dad if we need to call the ambulance. He doesn't answer and leans in close to me, his face only inches from mine.

"Jessie, we need to know what happened. Now."

I'm going to fall apart into tiny pieces, crumble right into the carpet, but when I speak, my voice comes out cold. Like I'm some kind of unfeeling psychopath. "I stabbed him. With a spear."

"What the hell?" Mother screams, but Dad only flinches. Like he's not all that surprised. His eyes lock on mine for a moment, and I can only imagine what he's thinking—Who is this monster? What happened to our daughter?—and then he grabs the bottle from Mother.

"Go get a blanket for Stephen," he barks. "He's shivering."

"We were spearfishing," I mutter. "It was an accident."

But no one is listening. Mother runs upstairs to get a blanket; Dad goes to the kitchen and comes back with a kitchen knife. He grabs the top of Stephen's boot. "Pull on this," he orders. "We need to cut the boot off, so we don't do more damage."

My hands are shaking, but I do my best to pull on the rubber while Dad slices down the boot. Then he yanks it away from me and continues cutting. I'm at a loss for what to do with myself, so I sink into the armchair and pull my knees up to my chest. Stephen groans and Mother places a blanket on him, tucking it gently under his chin.

"Don't worry," she whispers, touching her hand to his forehead. "Everything is going to be okay."

The boot lies in black shiny chunks on the rug, and when Dad moves back, I see what I have done.

Stephen's big toe is hanging abnormally low, and his sock is soaked with dark-red blood. My head feels strangely light and I want to cover my eyes, but I can't help myself: I lean closer.

"Sorry, buddy," Dad says, "but this is going to sting. We have no choice."

And when Dad reaches in to clean the wound, the gash I so gleefully made, my ears begin to ring and my stomach flips. I find myself on my feet, running for the kitchen sink. I make it just in time.

# Detachment

Stephen gets admitted quickly at emergency, and Dad and I hang out in the waiting room while Mother takes him in. We sit side by side, each flipping through a magazine, and I catch Dad looking at me every now and then with an odd look on his face. It's too soft to be anger. It could be disappointment, but there's something else mixed in with it. Pity maybe? The look seems to say, *I'm giving up, but I don't want to*. I almost tell him that I know exactly how he feels, that I feel the same way about myself, but I think if I try to speak I will break down and cry.

We're alone in the waiting room for the first half hour, and then an exhausted-looking woman with a crusty-nosed toddler comes in. She lowers herself onto one of the plastic chairs with a loud sigh and closes her eyes while her little boy tries to stack magazines on the top of his very black, very shiny hair. They fall off one by one, but he keeps on trying.

Dad puts his magazine down and closes his eyes. I wish he would say something, tell me everything is going to be all right. But he's probably thinking the same thing I am: what a loser the new Jessica Grenier has turned out to be. I've tried pretending I can be like the old Jessie, that I am as lovable and kind and as wonderful a friend/daughter/sister, but there's no point lying anymore.

Stephen. He's tried telling me, in his own sweet, nerdy way, to back off and give him space. But no, my defective brain couldn't—wouldn't—absorb something so simple. I stand up, and the room seems to shift under my feet.

"Jess?" Dad looks up at me. "Going somewhere?"

"Got a time machine?" I say. "We could travel back to this morning." I want to be funny, make him laugh, but I know my joke will fall flat. "Or better yet, three months ago."

Dad reaches up and puts his hand on my arm. "Jess," he says. "Let's not get into all this right now. It's late. It's been a long day. Let's just wait for your brother. Okay?"

The little boy is beside me then, tugging at my pant leg. "Gotta snack? Hey, lady. Gotta snack?"

"Lady?" I say. "Do I look like a lady?"

He gawks at me with huge brown eyes and nods. His mother shifts in her seat and gives us a quick look before closing her eyes again. "Excuse me," I say, and then again, louder: "Excuse me!" She opens her eyes and looks at me blankly. "Your little boy is hungry. Do you even give a crap?" Dad grabs my arm and pulls me down into the chair. The woman rolls her eyes and leans forward to dig in her purse.

"Jessie," he whispers. "Take it easy, please?"

I slump down. It's killing me, absolutely killing me, to be sitting here waiting. More than anything, I wish I could erase my idiotic fishing idea, make it all go away. And now Mother and Dad know about the party too, that I lied and made a total fool of myself. But all I can do is sit here and wait and accept that I am totally worthless.

We stay that way for another hour at least, the boy munching on crackers and then crashing on his mother's lap, before Mother comes through the doorway, her shoulders sagging. Her hair is a mess and she's all rumpled, like it's been days, not hours, since she's had a chance to glance in a mirror.

Dad stands up and they embrace in a long, tight hug.

"So?" Dad says. Mother leans on him; she has not yet looked my way. She'd rather pretend she has only one child, I'm sure.

"He's going to need surgery," she says, "to reattach the tendon. But first they need to get the swelling down. If everything goes smoothly, he'll be able to come home in a few days."

"Thank God," Dad says. A soft relief trickles through me, but it's not enough to take away the twisted feeling in my stomach.

Mother looks at me, her expression oddly neutral. "Stephen's asleep. Let's go home," she says.

We walk together in silence to the parking lot. It's dark and cold, and there is a full moon. No one says a word during the long drive home. When we finally turn off the highway to the gravel road that leads to our house, I clear my throat.

"I'm sorry," I say.

Mother glances back at me. "Okay," she says.

And the only other thing said is "good night" once we walk in our front door. Mother and Dad disappear to their room, to either collapse in exhaustion or discuss what they're going to do with their satanic daughter. I sit on my bed in the darkness. The clock reads *1:23*, but I know I cannot sleep, may never sleep again.

I click the light on and step up to the mirror. The Girl sizes me up, her lips pursed and her eyes narrow.

"Are you thinking what I'm thinking?" I whisper. She doesn't answer, but I see it in her eyes. We're on the same page, for once.

"I'm sorry I let you down," I say. I reach out and touch the glass with my fingertips. But I don't know why I bother. As always, I can't reach her.

At the back of the closet I find a backpack, which I fill with some clothes, my phone and charger, and a toothbrush. I grab the sand rose from my shelf, the printout of my photo collage and, for the Girl, the shoebox. Strangely calm, I make my way downstairs. I close the back door gently and step out into the night.

I can't be that Girl. I will always be only a second-rate version of the daughter and sister they adored. They're better off without me.

# Back to the Basics

I feel bad about it, but I chain Ginger to her doghouse so she won't follow me. She whimpers, and I rub her ears as I whisper, "Sorry, babe. Be a good girl. Take care of Stephen for me." I kiss the top of her head, then step away.

The trees sway in the wind, their trunks making cracking sounds, and my shoes crunch on the gravel. My body is tense, and I jerk at every strange noise, but I concentrate on following the beam of the flashlight on the ground, on breathing deeply and slowly. It won't be long before I'm at the camper.

Once past the bison pen and near the creek, I pick up my pace. I wish I could have taken Ginger with me. Every snapping branch has me swinging the flashlight around, searching for the reflection of some creature's eyes. The vastness of the night sky seems to swallow me up as I make my way down the path Tarin showed me. Inwardly, I beg the universe to please, please let this be the right way.

The wind whispers, telling me to hurry, to find my way before I am lost forever. Heart pounding, I focus on putting one foot in front of the other. And finally the trees open into a clearing and there it is, the moonlight reflecting off its metal walls. The camper.

I break into a run now. My pack thumps against my back as I get closer, and then I am standing at the door, out of breath. My hands tremble as I reach up and tug hard on the rusty little handle. The door pops open and I step inside, into pitch-blackness.

"Tarin?" I whisper. "You asleep?"

A few seconds pass, then a faint reply that's muffled by blankets: "Oh my god!" The camper sways a little and there are rustling sounds, and when my eyes adjust to the dark I can make out the outline of her, sitting on the upper bed. "I nearly peed my pants," she says. "You scared the hell out of me!"

I laugh, too loudly, with relief. I am here now, have made my choice. My pack slips off my back and onto the floor, and I let myself sink down after it. I am exhausted and exhilarated and terrified.

"That table turns into a bed, you know," Tarin says. "No need to crash on the floor."

I nod, which is dumb since she probably can't see me well from up there. She clicks on a flashlight and climbs down, the camper rocking again.

"We'll have to do a little safety check in the morning," she says. "Make sure we aren't going to flip this baby."

She props the flashlight on a shelf, then tugs at the tabletop, grunting, until she jerks back with it in her hands. She pulls out the metal tube it was propped on, then lays the tabletop between the two bench seats.

"Voilà," she says.

She offers me a hand, pulling me to my feet. We stand only a few inches apart. I'm guessing she is happy that I'm here—after all, she invited me—but I feel a bit awkward suddenly, like I am crashing her pajama party. She gestures to my new bed. "You didn't happen to bring a sleeping bag, did you?"

A simple question, but it hits me how little I've thought this out, that I should have actually taken the time to think about what I'll need to make it on my own.

"Crap," I say. It's surprisingly cool in the middle of the bush.

"Climb up top with me." Tarin steps onto my bed, and it creaks as she climbs back up to the bunk. "It'll be a little squished, but we can figure something out tomorrow." And what might that be? I nearly ask. Weaving a blanket out of some weeds? But I bite my tongue and follow her. I am determined to stay positive. We lie down in the cramped, musty-smelling space, and though she gives me half of her sleeping bag, I am still partly uncovered. I turn to face the door and close my eyes.

"Glad you're here," Tarin whispers.

"Me too," I answer. The jitters in my stomach, though, tell me it's too early to know for sure.

# Survival

So much for the tranquility of nature. It feels way too early when the sun breaks through the dingy curtains and the forest creatures start frolicking. I wrap my arm over my head, attempting to block out the squirrel chatter, but it's no use. I lie there, staring at a water stain on the ceiling that looks like Kermit the frog, until finally Tarin's groggy voice says, "Top of the morning to you."

I half roll, half fall off the mattress and onto the bed below. "I'm thirsty," I say.

Tarin's feet dangle above me as she pulls her legs over the side of the upper bed. "How about I whip you up a cappuccino?" Her laugh is a tight little snort.

Usually I am the first to play along with her sarcasm, but this morning it only makes me feel more tired. "You kill me," I say. She steps down beside me, then reaches under the table and pulls out a blue jug.

"Abracadabra." She opens a small cupboard above our heads and hands me a plastic cup. I lift the pitcher, but my hands tremble so much that I miss the cup, and water spills onto the bed.

"Whoa," she says. "You're shaky. And your aura is a weird gray color. I hope that's not from Mommy and Daddy withdrawal?"

I chug the water down. I'm a little wobbly, yes. Not exactly a prime candidate for Teenage Independent Living. She's going to have to take it easy on me, or she'll have a total mental case on her hands.

"I'm here, aren't I?" I say.

Her face softens. "Sorry, that was nasty. Honestly, I'm pretty surprised. I didn't expect you to show up."

"I didn't either," I say. "But things change."

Her look is boring right into my head, but I am not ready to tell her everything. I take another sip of water.

"Help me transform this bed back into the formal dining area," she says, "and I can dig you up some breakfast."

I am hungry. Between the spearfishing and the hospital last night, I missed dinner. We put the table back together, and then I squeeze in and get comfy. How quickly, I think, you could get to know someone living in such intimate quarters. And how well do I really know Tarin? I watch her pull out two tiny boxes of cereal from the cupboard and rip open a little door on the side of each.

"Cute," I say as she pours canned milk into the open sides of the cereal boxes.

"Yeah." She hands me my box, a plastic spoon sticking out of the side like she's stabbed it. "I couldn't resist these, even though they were out of my budget."

We polish them off in a few minutes, and I stand up to look for a place to put the garbage. Tarin pops the camper door open, and the brisk morning air and the scent of pine filters in.

"I didn't think of bringing any bags," she explains. "Maybe we can find a spot to use as our garbage dump, somewhere in the bush? Maybe beside our washroom facilities?"

Now that she mentions it, my bladder is uncomfortably full. "Do we have toilet paper?"

She nods and points toward a spot in the trees where something white hangs off a branch.

I make my way to the facilities, and when I'm done I stay in the woods a minute, watching the tips of the trees sway under the sky. I try not to think about it, but I can't help it: I wonder if they've noticed yet that I'm gone, if they've knocked on my door to get me up to head to the hospital to visit Stephen.

"Jessie!" Tarin calls. "Did you find the ladies' room?"

I ignore her, close my eyes and take a deep, deep breath. This is the best decision. It has to be.

"Jessie! Don't get lost out there!"

I tromp back to the clearing. When I walk up to the camper, Tarin is sitting outside on a log stump, a fuzzy orange poncho wrapped around her shoulders.

"I don't mean to be a control freak," she says. "I've wanted to do this for a long time, but now that I'm here, well"—she looks around, at the sky, at the trees, at me— "I'm bugging out a little."

"Hey," I say, "we're in this together." I'm surprised at the confident tone in my voice, but it seems to work. We exchange a high five, then look around, trying to think of what we should do next.

"Do we have any hunting and gathering to do?" I say.

"How about you tan the hides and I'll make some venison?"

We take in the woods in silence.

"Is your mom looking for you?" I ask. "Won't everyone be out scouring the area, especially when they discover I'm gone too?"

Tarin fiddles with the skull ring on her thumb. "I texted Mom that I was taking the bus back to the city to stay with an old friend for a few days. So no, she's not looking for me yet. She's probably happy I'm gone."

"Did you mention me?" I ask.

"No, but they might put two and two together. Let's make sure the location services are shut off on your phone. Then text your parents and say you're meeting me.

That way, they probably won't look anywhere local. And by the time they do, we'll be long gone."

"Gone? Where are we going?"

Tarin laughs. "Hey, save something to talk about later. I'm going to tidy up our crib." She goes back inside the camper, slamming the door behind her. I can't imagine what there is to do, except maybe fold the sleeping bag. I take her spot on the stump, close my eyes and breathe in the cool air while she bustles about inside our home.

Starting fresh, I tell myself. A new beginning.

# Intruder

Tarin and I fill the rest of the day by cracking lame jokes, peeing in the bush, eating tiny amounts of food, so as not to use up our cache, and napping, staying as close to the camper as possible. I know I should ask her again about the plan, but what's the hurry? So much has happened already, it's easier to live this way, moment to moment.

I get my phone out, and Tarin shuts off my tracking. I text Mother and Dad. Meeting up with Tarin. Don't worry. Tell Stephen I'm sorry. I take a few photos of the woods, the squirrels, the sky. But my heart is not in it. I keep picturing Mother and Dad at the police station, clutching a photo of me; Dad driving around in his old blue pickup, looking for signs of me. It weighs on me, knowing I am putting them through another drama. Or maybe they're so mad they don't even care.

That night it gets so freezing cold that Tarin and I huddle together, shivering, under the thin sleeping bag.

When the soft light of early morning finally comes, Tarin begins to snore. I wrap my arms around my head, but then I hear loud thumps coming from outside the camper door. I sit up quickly and whack my head on the low ceiling.

"Tarin," I whisper. "Someone's out there."

She opens her eyes a slit, then shuts them again. "It's probably a squirrel," she mumbles.

The clunk comes again, louder, and Tarin's eyes snap open.

"That's some monster squirrel," I say. She sits up beside me and clutches my arm. We hold our breath, listening. Nothing.

"Maybe it was—" Another thump, this time closer. I grab on to her too, and we stare at each other, eyes wide open, waiting helplessly for something—we don't know what, but it will be horrible—to happen. We wait and wait like that, our faces so close I can feel her breath. Then our grips start to relax, and we pull slowly away from each other.

I let go of her hands and lower myself over the edge of the bed. Tarin sucks in her breath as I reach for the door handle and push until the door pops open.

The grass sparkles with dew. I don't see anything, but my mind makes all kinds of crazy leaps: a creature of some kind, maybe a cougar, has climbed onto the roof and is waiting to pounce on us; a Sasquatch is throwing stones at the camper; a plane has dropped us a bag of supplies—thank God, because we're already running low on toilet paper.

"Jess?" Tarin asks softly. "What is it?"

"I don't see—" But then I do. There, on the edge of the bush, the backside of something big and brown disappears into the canopy of trees. I'm actually relieved.

"A bear," I say. "It's just a bear."

The camper rocks as Tarin gets down and peers out the door. "Just? *Just* a bear?" She's trying to whisper, but her voice is high. "A real one?"

"No," I say, "it was Winnie-the-Pooh. Of course it was real." I want to tell her to get a grip already, but I bite my tongue. She's a city girl. "It was probably only curious, checking out the camper."

"Or looking for breakfast."

I don't know if she sees me roll my eyes, but she plops down at the table and rests her chin in her hands. She looks helpless and forlorn.

"Speaking of breakfast," I say, sitting down opposite her, "do we have anything?"

She sighs. "Well, not bacon or eggs or anything. But we have some canned ham left, and some Kraft dinner."

My stomach does a flip. "No more Lucky Charms?"

She shakes her head. "I finished them off last night."

A feeling of dread grips me. I didn't bring food and haven't contributed to our survival in any way. Maybe I'm not being fair, but I'd assumed Tarin had all the details worked out. She promised me an escape, not starvation.

The honeymoon is officially over.

"Don't worry, my princess," she says. "There'll be plenty of food soon enough."

"Is that right?" I say. "And where is it going to come from? Are little elves going to make a delivery?"

She waves her hand in front of her, signaling me to stop. "I have a plan. If you'd let me talk, maybe I could explain."

Let her talk? She's had more than ample opportunity to spill the beans. When she smiles across the table at me with an odd, crooked grin, it hits me why she hasn't spoken up—she's nervous. Tarin, Miss Screw-the-World-and-Who-Gives-a-Shit-What-Anybody-Thinks, actually cares about my opinion.

"My boyfriend is on his way to get us—he'll be here any day now. Could arrive any minute, really. We have to hang in there, be patient."

"Your boyfriend?" I say. "Won't your mom think of looking for him? Won't that mess things up?"

She shakes her head. "My mom's never met him," she says. "She doesn't even know about him." She's looking down at her hands, cleaning her nails, and it hits me: she's hiding something.

"Have *you* ever met him?" And the way she keeps looking down, I know the answer immediately.

"Oh my god," I say. "You've never met him. He's some guy you met online, and he could be a complete psycho."

Her head whips up and her eyes narrow. "Falcon is not psycho," she snaps. "He's the kindest, sweetest guy ever. You'll see."

"Falcon?" My voice is shrill. "What kind of name is Falcon?"

She shakes her head, as if I am the one who's an idiot. "It's a nickname, obviously."

Super Doc's counting technique is about to fail me. "And what's his real name?"

"I can't remember," she answers. "But who cares? He's awesome, he's got a car, and he's willing to drive all the way from the coast to help us out. These are the important details."

"You're kidding, right?" I've watched the TV movies of the week, seen all the cop shows. I may be brain-damaged, but I am not totally out to lunch. Tarin looks at me, her eyes framed by black eyeliner, waiting. Waiting for me to freak out. And I want to. I want to scream at her, tell her it's all her fault that I have nowhere to turn. Strangely, though, staring back at her, with her dirty hair and clothes, looking a little scared—of me—something inside of me shuts down.

Yes, I am mad. And freaked out. But part of me lets it all go, lets this awful feeling of being completely alone sink deep into my very core.

"Look," Tarin says, "it sounds crazy, I know. But I've known him for almost six months, and you trust me, right? Anyway, it's not like we have many other options."

She's right about that. But it's a lot to take in, and I need time alone to absorb it all. I stand up and reach under the table for my backpack.

"I'll be back soon," I say. I push the door open and step outside, letting the door slam shut behind me.

I don't think. My feet move, one in front of the other, toward the trees that sway gently in the breeze.

# Outsider

I don't glance back to see if Tarin has opened the camper door, if she's trying to stop me from leaving. All I want to do is find a spot in the wild grass, or among the leaves and branches in the bush, and curl up in a ball. I want to feel sorry for myself, wallow in self-pity. My life sucks. It isn't fair, what's happened to me. Even Dr. K. said so.

I wonder if the bear is somewhere nearby, waiting for me to let down my guard so he can eat me. Perfect, I think. Saves me having to think about what to do with myself.

Tarin is as lost and confused as I am; I can't really expect her to be my savior. But a guy she met online? It's kind of pathetic. The harsh reality, though, is that if I don't go with her and this Falcon dude, I'm doomed. I know from my failed attempt at spearfishing that I'm not exactly qualified to live off Mother Nature's bounty. I make my way toward the creek, and when I reach the bank I see the footprints Stephen and I made, still there deep in the mud. I take out my phone and click a few shots, then turn it off and put it back in my pack.

My stomach growls and I remember—I haven't had my cereal. The thought of eating canned mushy ham makes me want to barf. As I walk and the fresh air fills my lungs, an idea forms in my mind. Mother and Dad must be heading to the hospital soon, since Stephen is supposed to be there for a few days. If the coast is clear, maybe I can sneak into the house and grab a stash of Lucky Charms.

It's daring and maybe a little careless, but I'm pumped up from the fight with Tarin. I march, determined, until I reach the bison pen, then past the shed where Stephen and I played Pygmies. I slow my pace, take deep breaths and stay on the edge of the trees. Ginger could start barking and blow my cover. Before I come up with a plan for that, though, she's there beside me, her tail thumping against my leg. Leaning down, I rub behind her ears and give her a kiss on the top of the head. "That's my girl," I whisper.

It's so quiet. Maybe Dad and Mother have already left. I'm about to step onto the back stairs that lead to the kitchen when a scraping sound—a chair across the floor maybe?—makes me freeze. I duck and creep carefully to the trees outside the side window, where I dip below the branches and bring my knees up to my chest. Ginger curls up beside me and closes her eyes.

I pull myself closer to the tree trunk as a shape appears in the window. It's Mother, in her housecoat. She steps closer to the glass, staring off into the distance somewhere above the trees. She wraps her arms tightly around herself, and then Dad is there too. He kisses her softly on the cheek, then takes her hand and leads her away from my view.

Sadness settles over me. She's always tried her hardest, my mother. There may be a stiffness to her sometimes, which I'm clueless how to read, but that's just who she is. They're good people, my parents, and I wish I hadn't let them down. I've let Stephen down too, and Dr. K. I wonder if she knows, if she's worried about me. I didn't even do my last homework assignment—to write about my idea of the perfect life. *Describe it to me*, she'd said.

I can't go in the house yet, but I'm not ready to go back and face Tarin. Maybe Dr. K. will never see it, but my assignment was meant to help me figure things out. If I am trying to start fresh, I need a vision of what I imagine my future to be. And this cosy nook under the tree, with Ginger by my side, is as good a place as any to get started. I pull my notebook and pen out of my backpack.

*My Perfect Life*, I write. I peer up at the window, near where Mother and Dad must be sitting, drinking their morning coffee, then scribble down what comes to mind. *A nice family. People who love me. Being myself. Taking photos. Having friends that I choose. Making decisions about my life on my own. Feeling like I belong.*

It's not eloquent, and I'm surprised that I have nothing else to say. Is the secret to my happiness legitimately that simple? And why didn't I add *memories of my old life* to that list? It came to my mind. I'm chewing on the end of the pen, thinking, when a car door slams and Ginger leaps up and bolts across the lawn, barking. I listen to Mother and Dad drive away.

After Ginger comes back I wait a few minutes to be sure the coast is clear, then creep out of my hiding spot and up the steps. In the kitchen, I am all business, filling a bag with food. In the basement, I open the closet in the spare bedroom to look for blankets and find a sleeping bag tied up with twine. There's also a small camouflage duffel bag with binoculars and a set of camping dishes in it, so I take that too. I don't look around, don't linger, don't let myself get sentimental.

Outside, I give Ginger a good rub, then order her to stay. She obeys, watching with droopy eyes as I go. I pull out my phone and take two shots: one of her, one of the house. I walk away from the life that once was and could have been, back toward the cut line. My body is stiff, and my throat tight and dry.

Tarin is not at the camper when I make it back. I scarf down some cereal, crawl up to the bunk, bury myself in the sleeping bag that smells like home and fall asleep.

# Road Trip

The top of the camper is hot and stuffy, and I wake up to the sound of voices.

"Dude," a deep one says, "this is a pretty sweet joint."

A laugh—Tarin's—then: "You don't have to say that. It's not great, but it's served its purpose."

"Hey, beats sleeping in the back of a car."

I peer out from the sleeping bag and see a guy with spiky orange hair standing by the door with Tarin. Something dark, thin and furry sits on his shoulder, staring up at me with beady eyes. I haven't had time to think about Tarin and our fight. I want to hide a little longer, but the smell of that little beast tickles my nose, and I sneeze. Tarin glances up at me.

"Jess," she says. "I thought maybe you'd backed out on me."

I pull myself out of the sleeping bag. "Not exactly," I say. The guy extends his hand upward, and I shake it limply.

"Falcon," he says. "*Enchanté.*"

"Jessica," I say.

He rubs the weaselly thing—I think it's a ferret—under its chin. "And this is sweet little Lady Di."

Tarin and I share a look, and I can see in her eyes that she's glad I'm back. "Do we have any Coke or anything?" I say. "I'm parched."

"Whoa, you look too innocent for the hard stuff," Falcon says, and the ferret nuzzles his neck. Tarin whacks his shoulder with a playful punch.

"You goof," she says. "She means Coca-Cola. You know, the beverage."

"Whew," he says, and I see the shimmer of a stud on his tongue when he talks. "Don't want to be around junk like that. I take care of myself, stay away from the bad stuff. You know, my body is my temple and all that jazz."

"We only have water," Tarin says as I climb down to the table.

"No problemo," Falcon says. "We'll make a pit stop and get some road pops. Some good tunes, snacks, and we'll be ready to hit the highway."

I clear my throat. "We're leaving?"

"Did you think we were going to stay here forever? Eat bark and grow old together?" Tarin says.

"Of course not," I say. "But now? I mean, already?"

"Pack up, little lady," Falcon says. "We leave in five."

It doesn't take long—all I've got is my backpack, sleeping bag and the camouflage duffel—but I stay in the camper, taking deep breaths despite the smell, while they chat outside, until Falcon yells at me to get my butt in gear already. I'm freaked out and not sure what I'm doing, but I don't have a plan B, so I follow them past the camper and through the woods a way we haven't gone before.

Falcon whistles what sounds like "I'm a Little Teapot" as we walk. I stay behind them, and after ten minutes or so we reach the gravel road. It must be the same road that goes past my house and Tarin's grandmother's, but farther along.

A beat-up yellow car sits on the side of the road, nearly in the ditch.

"Your chariot awaits," Falcon says with a wink.

"We'll go the long way back to the highway," Tarin says, opening the front door, "so no one sees us."

I climb in the back, and the car sputters a few times before it finally starts. Falcon gooses the engine, and we take off with a skid down the road. Music blares out of the speakers, and Falcon sings along: *Light 'em up up up, light 'em up up up, I'm on fire!*

We hit a bump in the road and a loud scraping sound comes from under the seat. Nervous energy flows through me, and I need to channel it somewhere. I zip open the camo duffel bag I took from the basement. I didn't have time to fully check out its contents, to see how equipped I am to start my new life. There are the binoculars and set of plastic dishes, and tucked under that I discover a

Swiss Army knife. I pull the blades out one by one, then the little scissors and corkscrew. Falcon glances in the rearview mirror. "Sweet," he yells over the music. "I had one of those when I was a kid!"

I close the knife and put it in my pocket—at least I have a weapon if he does turn out to be psycho—then unzip a smaller compartment at one end of the bag. Reaching inside, my hand meets something smooth and cool. When I pull it out, I'm surprised to see a camera. It's an older one, but with a substantial lens attached to the front. I don't have the expertise to tell if it's good quality or not, but it's heavy and looks like the real deal.

I push the Power button and the screen lights up.

The music fades at the end of the song. "Jess," Tarin says, "what do you want to listen to? Eminem or some classic Nirvana?"

"Whatever," I say.

The music goes up a notch, so loud I feel the vibration of the beat through the seat. I push some buttons on the front of the camera—the center of a round dial, one with an arrow on it—until a photo appears on the screen.

It's an off-center close-up of the Girl, the top right of her head not in the frame. She has a steely look in her eyes, not even a hint of a smile. It's another selfie, but this one was not taken in her room. Behind her there are trees and sky. And around her face, like the hood of a medieval cape, is the red scarf I found in Stephen's drawer.

In the left corner of the picture are two wooden posts. I can barely make out the thin lines stretched between them. It's a section of a fence, and I've only seen one like it on the farm. It's part of the bison pen.

"This is so exciting!" Tarin yells. "Yahoo!"

A fluttery feeling grows in my stomach. The date at the bottom of the photo is April 26.

Tarin and Falcon rock out in the front seat. "*This is,*" they sing, "*survival of the fittest, this is do or die...*" But I'm not listening. My mind races through all the clues I have gathered these past weeks about who the Girl was. The part in the Girl's journal, after Harrison called her Most Likely to Be Wearing Old Lady Underwear, about not wanting to be boring. *Maybe one day I'll work up the guts to do something crazy...* Hands trembling, I put the camera in the bag, then take out my phone and get onto Facebook.

The night before the Very Bad Day, she posted the quote-and-flower photo. *And the day came when the risk to remain tight in a bud was more painful than the risk it took to blossom.* And the post before that is the photo of the girl with long blond hair lying casually across the back of a tiger, as though it's a piece of plush furniture. Loosely tied around her neck is a red scarf.

The caption under the photo reads *Cutting-Edge Photos with Wild Animals.* I click on the link and discover a whole album, dozens of photos of girls and women in romantic clothing, surrounded by woods. In some, the forest is foggy and dark, creating an eeriness; in others, the leaves on the trees are crisp in the daytime light. The models pose with animals you wouldn't usually see in photos with humans: one girl with shocking-red hair has her arms wrapped around a bear; a skinny brunette sits in front of an elephant, its trunk wrapped around her waist; the same blond from the tiger photo leans against a caribou. The photos are surreal and amazing and very, very daring.

The music fades from the speakers. "J, my lady!" Falcon yells back at me. "You gotta loosen up, let your hair down. Didn't you get the memo? Road trips are supposed to be fun, man."

I don't answer. My mind scrambles to fill in the missing details. The scarf. The camera. Dad didn't say anything about seeing them when he found me in the pen. Why would he leave that out?

And then it hits me like slap in the face—I know who must have the answers. But the farther we travel down the road, the closer we get to our fresh start, the greater the distance between me and the truth.

I have to do it now, before it's too late. "Let me out," I say.

"What?" Tarin peers back at me. "What did you say?"

"Let me out," I say again, loud and slow.

"You gotta pee already?" Falcon says, the car veering to the side of the road.

"No."

A feeling comes over me, something strange and powerful. It's not exactly me, or the me of recent memory, who's talking. It's the girl I used to be, the girl I am now and the girl I will become, all rolled into one. They're in agreement, coming together for the first time. It surprises me and at the same time makes me feel strong. And whole.

"No, I don't have to pee," I say. "Just stop the car."

Falcon slows down, and he and Tarin exchange a look.

More than anything, I want to get out. I don't want to go on a road trip to God-knows-where with a stinky ferret. I want to go home.

I detach my seat belt and clutch onto the back of Falcon's seat. "I said, stop the car!" He actually laughs as the car skids to a halt, pieces of gravel dinging the underside of the car like popcorn in a pot.

He turns and looks at me with an amused expression. "All right, all right. Chill already."

Tarin, though, doesn't look so amused. "Jess." Her voice is tight, careful, but her eyes are wild with panic. "What's going on?"

I don't let her unnerve me. "I'm not coming," I say. "I made a mistake."

Falcon sighs loudly and rests his head on the steering wheel. "Chicks. So much drama."

He doesn't seem like such a bad guy, but I doubt he's the ticket to whatever it is we're looking for. I turn to Tarin and lean in closer to talk softly.

"You can change your mind too," I say. "It's not too late. Maybe you can talk to your mom. Tell her how you feel."

She leers at me, arms across her chest. She's trying to be tough, but I see it in her eyes: she wants me to convince her, to find those magic words that will make her believe we don't need to run. I don't have the words yet for this feeling that's building inside me. So I use the words that had inspired the Girl.

"I read a quote the other day," I say slowly, the thought unraveling in my mind, "that said"—I'm not sure I have it, but then the Girl helps me out—"that said, *The day came when the risk to remain tight in a bud was more painful than the risk it took to blossom.*" Tarin looks at me like I've gone off the deep end. "All right, it's kind of hokey. But I think it's about taking a chance, about not being afraid to open up to life, to other people. Things are a little screwed up for us, I know. But maybe we need to try harder to make things better, instead of blaming everyone else."

She grips her hands tightly in her lap. The ferret makes a weird squeaking noise; Falcon has his head tilted back and his eyes closed. My rambling probably didn't make a bit of sense, but I know what I feel is real. We are not doomed. There are people who care about us, love us, and even if it's not a bed of roses, it's got to be better than nothing.

Tarin closes her eyes, and I think I might have gotten through to her, made her feel a twinge of hope. But when she opens them again, I see that stubborn look of hers. I have lost.

"God, Jess, don't be a wimp," she snaps. "You're not happy at home, you know that. They don't know you, the real you. This is your chance for freedom, and you're blowing it."

I look at her long and hard, and then do the surest thing I ever remember doing. I open the side door, grab my camera and bags, and step out onto the road.

"Thanks anyway, Falcon," I say, and I close the door.

The car moves slowly forward at first, then spits gravel behind it as it picks up speed. I watch it leave, my backpack hanging in one hand, the duffel bag in the other. I am nervous about facing my family. But I feel so alive that I let out a loud scream.

There is no one there to hear, only open fields stretching out on either side of me. But I am there, and I hear it, and I feel it, too, deep inside. And that counts for something.

I begin the long walk home.

# Filling in the Blanks

I'm sweaty and my legs ache by the time I see the chimney of our house poking through the trees. Tarin and Falcon and Lady Di are probably far down the highway by now, have probably moved on to Nirvana.

The wind moves the pines softly, and it's quiet around the house. I stand there a few minutes and look at it, this little corner of the world that is ours, and it washes through me finally. Real gratitude. It's a good place, and even if I may not always feel I belong, it is my home too. Everyone may miss the old Jessica. But I think they might be willing to give the new one—me—a chance too.

Ginger motors across the lawn, tail wagging so fast she looks like she could become airborne.

"Baby doll," I say, and she dives into me, rubbing her face on my legs and letting out a soft whine as I massage her ears. "Don't worry."

There's no car parked at the end of the driveway. I walk slowly up to the door. It's not locked. Inside, I grab the phone and dial Mom's cell. It rings a few times and then her voice mail comes on.

"Mom," I say. "It's me. I'm home. " My voice cracks. "I'll be here, waiting."

It hits me when I hang up: I didn't call her Mother. And it came out naturally, without any effort.

I pace around the house, jittery and hungry and exhausted. I can't stand the waiting, so I fill a bowl with cereal and milk but can only eat half of it. My phone dings, and when I pick it up, I have a text: `Hello pretty pixie. Hope you don't mind I got your number through some connections. I am a very powerful ogre, you know. Wanted to say sorry. Shouldn't have let you touch that nasty potion. How are things out in the wilds?`

Ogre. It's Dan, the guy from the pit party. I can't help smiling. But I am not ready to write back, have no idea when I will feel normal enough to go down that road. Ginger barks outside, and I hear car doors closing. First things first.

I stand at the top of the steps. Dad sees me and bounds up the stairs, then throws his arms around me so tight I can barely breathe. Mom comes behind him, and she's hugging me, tears making a trail down her cheeks. Dad lets go, runs back down the stairs and gets Stephen, with his crutches, and plunks him beside me. Then we are all wrapping our arms around each other in a twisted human pretzel.

"I'm sorry," I say. "I'm so, so sorry."

When we finally pull apart, Dad says, "Where the hell have you been?"

We sit around the kitchen table and I tell them everything: that Tarin and I didn't take the bus anywhere, and that we were not so far away at all. I tell them about the camper, and how I couldn't stand myself for hurting Stephen. How sorry I was.

Dad shakes his head. "We've been out of our minds with worry. I can't believe you were so close all this time. The police have been looking for you in the city, visiting all of Tarin's friends."

Mom looks at me with red eyes. "Don't ever do that to us again."

I nod and squeeze her hand on the table. "Never," I say, and I turn to Stephen. "And I hope you can forgive me, one day, for stabbing your foot."

"Well," he says, "we're not letting you around the kitchen knives for a long, long time."

And when I look at them, the three people who love me most in the world, I know that if we are going to make this work, really be a family, it's time to put everything out in the open. I take a deep breath.

"I learned something while I was gone. About what happened with Ramses."

Mom and Dad look surprised. "Did you remember?" Mom says.

I shake my head. "I found a photo."

"Photo?" Dad says. "Of what?"

"A selfie I took. Standing in front of the pen. I think maybe it was right before I got hurt."

Mom and Dad glance at each other, and Stephen stares down at the table. "But," Dad says, "you didn't have your phone with you. That doesn't make sense."

"It was on a camera I found in the basement," I say. "And I found this too." I reach into the duffel bag and unfold the red scarf, smoothing it with my hands on the middle of the table.

Stephen lifts his head, his face twisted in confusion. "What are you doing?" he says, his voice trembling. "Why are you doing this?"

"I need to understand, Stephen," I say.

A shudder goes through Little Man's body, like a huge pressure has been building inside and he can't keep it there anymore. "But when you woke up, in the hospital," he says, his voice high and shaky, "I tried to talk to you about what happened. You said we never needed to talk about it again, that it didn't matter."

He looks at me with so much desperation, I feel it clutching at me. "I'm sorry, Stephen," I say. "I only said that because I was tired, and you looked so upset. Please, Little Man. Help me out."

"What," Dad says, his voice sharp and impatient, "are you two talking about?"

Stephen lets out a long, deep sigh. And I feel it coming. Finally, the moment of truth. "I know what happened to Jessica."

Mom's hand flies to her mouth. "What? How?"

"I know," Stephen says, "because I was there."

Dad slams his hand on the table. "You were in the pen too?"

Stephen nods, then turns to face me. "At first," he says slowly, "in the house, I went along with your plan. You said you wanted to play fashion shoot. That I could be a famous photographer taking photos of a movie star. Pierre, you called me. You said photos in front of the bison would be cool. I had to go to the bathroom, so I said I'd meet you at the pen."

I nod for him to go on.

"But then, when I got there, you were opening the gate. When I asked what you were doing, you said the fence would ruin the pictures. You had that dumb scarf around your head and said you wanted something more artistic. You wanted to lie in the hay, stretched out, with the bison in the background. You told me what *avant-garde* meant. I said that it was too risky, but you said the bison knew you, that they trusted you. You looked me in the eye and said, *I need to do this, Stephen. Promise me that you will never, ever tell. This will be our secret, to carry to the grave.* I said I didn't want to, that I was going to run and get Mom and Dad."

"So," Mom says, "why didn't you?"

Little Man wraps his arms around himself. "I had never seen your face like that. You looked so determined—almost angry. *We always look out for each other*, you said. *I always have your back, now you have to cover mine.* You said that if I couldn't keep your secret, you couldn't keep mine." He freezes, his face contorting with emotion. He struggles to keep it in, but a sob wracks his body. "You said," he chokes out, "that you would tell Mom and Dad what *I* had done."

I don't get it for a few seconds as I watch him put his head down on his folded arms. Mom gets up and puts her arms around him. But then the thought gets clearer in my mind: the old Jessica had something on him, something he was scared to get in trouble for. The Girl blackmailed him. Not exactly nice behavior from Miss Sweet-as-Candy.

"I swear," I say gently, "I have no idea what you did. And even if I did remember, I wouldn't rat you out."

Mom lets him out of her embrace and he sits up, rubbing his face on his sleeve. "It's all right," he says. "I was going to tell the truth about everything anyway. How I was looking down at the camera, trying to figure out the buttons. I heard a thumping on the ground and when I looked up, Ramses came charging out of nowhere. I yelled at you to run, but you tripped on a rock. Your scarf went flying. And then Ramses was there. I felt so helpless. I grabbed the scarf—I don't know why. Then I ran to get help. But when I was on my way to the house, Dad found you. I could hear him yelling from the pen, and when I reached the front door, I told Mom you were hurt. I was going to confess everything, and I didn't care if I got into trouble or if you told my secret."

He lets out a long breath. "But then I saw you lying there in the hospital, all beat up. I knew you might die, that I might never talk to you again. And I couldn't break our promise. You were right." He smiles weakly at me. "We've always had each other's backs. So I hid the camera and the scarf. I didn't know you had taken a selfie before I got to the pen, or I would have erased it."

I smile back at him, and my eyes water. Oh, Little Man. What hell the Girl has put him through: the weight of his secret, a crazy sister and the farm going up for sale. All this for some artsy photos to prove she could do something daring, different. My mind goes over the past few weeks. Stephen's strange behavior when I asked him about the Very Bad Day. The feeling I had that he blamed me for Mom and Dad wanting to sell the farm. Even small things, like his frustration when I wanted to drive the quad. *Who's going to know?* I had said. And his answer: *I will. You will. Isn't that enough?* So many things make sense now.

But Stephen is not done. He turns to face Mom and Dad. "One day when you weren't home, I did something really stupid and dangerous. I broke into the gun cabinet, and I took out Dad's shotgun." Little Man's face flushes red, but he shows courage and carries on. "I went out back and put shells in it, like Dad showed me, and I shot at some cans. I was careful, and everything was fine. But then, on my last shot, Ginger came popping out of nowhere, and the bullet almost hit her." His eyes well up and his body goes limp. "I could have killed her. It was horrible." He looks at me now, and the guilt I see in his eyes clenches a fist around my heart.

A heavy silence hangs in the room. Then Dad stands up. He goes around the table and wraps his arms around Stephen. Little Man looks deflated. "We will definitely be talking about this more later," he says. "But for now, thank you for telling the truth."

"Stephen," Mom says. "Our dear, dear Stephen." And she runs her fingers gently across his forehead and into his hair.

My little bro suffered through this for a sister I had thought was so damn perfect. I should hate the Girl, should march into the bathroom and tell her what I think of her. That she's a blackmailer and a manipulator. That her need to prove she could do something interesting was pathetic, and she should be ashamed. But despite all that, I'm not one tiny bit angry. She didn't have it all figured out either. Like me, she was trying desperately to be her own person without disappointing the people she cared about. All this time I've been cowering under her shadow, trying to live up to an ideal that wasn't even real. A feeling of serenity comes over me, a melting away of all the pressure I've been carrying around the past weeks.

"Geez," I say, "I used to be a horrible jerk. But don't worry—brain damage has fixed me all up."

Stephen lets out a choked laugh, and, surprisingly, Mom and Dad laugh too.

---

After our big talk, I call Tarin's mother and give her all the information I have on Falcon. I hope Tarin won't hate me, but I think—I hope—that if her mother would show Tarin she cares, genuinely cares, they can make things better. I get off the phone and a tidal wave of fatigue hits me. I am on my way to the stairs when I pause in the doorway of the living room, where Mom and Dad sit holding hands on the couch.

"Mom? Dad?" I say. "Do you think maybe we could reconsider the decision to sell the farm, if it's not too late?"

They share a look. Mother nods slowly. "There are still a few conditions pending before the sale is final. So I suppose we could talk about it."

It's enough for me, for now.

Upstairs, I pay a visit to Stephen's room. He looks exhausted too.

"I have one last thing to confess," he says. "Don't laugh at me, but every time I missed you when you were in the coma, I slept with that scarf." His cheeks flush a deep pink. "I know. I'm a dork."

"No," I say. "You're the best." And I squeeze him so hard he lets out a squeal.

Then I collapse on my bed and drift off. It's not quite as deep as the Big Sleep I began on April 26, but it's pretty darn close.

# The Olive Branch

I wake up early the next morning, and the house is quiet. I sneak down to the basement, connect the camera to the computer and download the selfie the Girl took seconds before everything changed. The Girl's face, *my* face, is calm on the screen, youthful and innocent. Seeing her there, I feel a little sad but hopeful too. I lift my phone and take a new selfie, then email it to myself.

Once I have both selfies in the photo-editing program, I manipulate their colors—bright orange, some lime green in the backdrop. I place them side by side and surround them with a thick black frame. It's perfect. Me and the Girl. Not entirely different, but not exactly the same either.

I save the image as Us, and then write a text to Tarin.

Please don't be mad. I want to be your friend, but I couldn't live with myself if you got hurt.

The next one is for Megan.

Hello BFF. I know I haven't been easy to be around. Can I have another chance? No cupcakes, I promise.

There's Ogre, too, to answer eventually. And also the email from the TBI support group that might be worth checking out. But more urgent, there is someone else I need to talk to before I can truly start again.

Downstairs, I throw on my plaid coat and step outside into the chilly morning air. Ginger follows as I make my way to the bison pen. The herd is partway out to the field, but when I call, a few cows gallop over toward the fence. Behind them, the obvious king of the herd emerges. It's Ramses, and he makes his way more slowly, his head down. He doesn't get as close to the fence as the cows, but he's looking toward me, waiting.

"I came to make peace," I say. "I don't hate you for what happened. I was in your space, I know. You're the boss, and you were probably doing what you felt was right to protect your family. I can't blame you for that."

He lets out a snort and paws at the ground.

"So how about it?" I say. "Do you think there's room for both of us out here?"

Another snort, and he turns and gallops off into the herd, sending a few young bulls trotting away from the bales. I lean on the fence and watch them for a few minutes, and the tiniest bit of warmth rises up inside of me. Jessica loved them, and maybe I can learn to, at least a little.

In the house, everyone is still sleeping, so I go back up to my room. The Girl is waiting there for me.

"Good morning," I say, "my friend."

She looks worn out, but there is a glint of hope in her tired eyes.

"Stop beating yourself up over it," I say. "You're only human." She leans in closer, and I know she is listening. Finally.

"We've been through a lot together, haven't we?" I say. "I know I've been a nightmare to deal with. But whether we like it or not, we've built this life together."

And then I take a deep breath and work up the guts to do something I can no longer put off: ask her to step aside. "Do you think I can do it, make it all work, on my own? I'm ready to try. The big question is, are you willing to let me?"

Her lips curl up into a gentle smile that spreads slowly to the rest of her face. For the first time outside of photos from before the Very Bad Day, I see that got-my-whole-life-ahead-of-me grin. At the same time, the Girl seems to be fading somehow, the image in the glass growing fainter.

Now, when I look at her, I see a little bit of myself too.

I might never get all my past back, I know. The memories may stay stubbornly stuck in the shadows of my mind forever. Or they may come back to me in bits and pieces, or in one huge wave when I least expect it. Whatever the future brings, I owe it to both of us to give this life of ours a real shot.

Because I do remember. I remember everything that's happened to me since I came out of the Big Sleep, and how wrong it felt to be away from home. Most of all, I remember how, when Mom, Dad and Stephen wrapped their arms tightly around me, a feeling of warmth, of what must be love, flooded over me and filled me up.

And maybe this is the only memory that matters.

# Author's Note

What happened to Jessica in *Blank* is fiction. Writing her story was a way for me to explore unanswered questions I had after completing a degree in psychology, such as how chemical reactions in the brain shape personality and what role memory plays in the development of our sense of self. There are, however, millions of people around the world who face the very real challenges of living with Traumatic Brain Injury (TBI). In the United States, about 1.7 million TBIs occur each year, with 52,000 resulting in death. In Canada, approximately 2.4 percent of the population sustained a head injury in 2009–2010. TBI is shockingly common. *

The main causes of brain injury are sudden jolts or blows to the head during sports and recreational activities, motor vehicle collisions, falls, acts of violence and workplace accidents. The effects of TBI can include fatigue, impaired speech and motor control, cognitive challenges, hearing and memory loss, headaches, difficulty managing emotions, seizures and myriad other symptoms. Every case of TBI is unique, and unfortunately, there are no easy fixes.

While the retrograde amnesia Jessica faces in the story is very rare, it's not merely a cliché. People around the world have shared their personal stories of struggling with this kind of amnesia, in books and documentaries. One such account is *The Man Who Lost Himself: The Terry Evanshen Story*, by June Callwood. Terry is a retired CFL player who lost all memory of his past after a car accident but was able to rebuild his life with the support of his family. Captain Trevor Greene, a Canadian peacekeeper who suffered a TBI in Afghanistan, also shared his story, in a documentary called *Peace Warrior*. Though I can't pretend to understand what having TBI or amnesia is like, such inspiring stories helped me do my job as a writer and try to put myself in their shoes.

Many organizations exist to help if you or a loved one is dealing with brain injury. The Brain Association of Canada can be found at http://biac-aclc.ca/, and the Brain Association of America at http://www.biausa.org/.

Please take care of your brain. Wear a helmet when biking, skateboarding, skiing and playing contact sports, and always wear a seat belt. For more information, check out www.protectyourhead.com.

**\* Sources:**

Centers for Disease Control and Prevention. "Traumatic Brain Injury in the United States: Fact Sheet." http://www.cdc.gov/traumaticbraininjury/get_the_facts.html
Statistics Canada. "Injuries in Canada: Insights from the Canadian Community Health Survey." http://www.statcan.gc.ca/

# Acknowledgments

Thank you to all the teachers who inspired me to love books and the act of creating with words, from elementary teachers in Wandering River to the faculty of the Vermont College MFA program. Thanks, too, to my graduating class (the Zoo) for giving me a sense of belonging in a fantastic community of writers, and special kudos to Shen for her help and encouragement with *Blank*.

Much appreciation also to all my friends and family members over the years who listened to or read my stories, asked about my writing or told me not to give up. You know who you are. It meant a lot.

A huge thank-you to Andrew Wooldridge and everyone at Orca Book Publishers for taking *Blank* on, particularly Sarah Harvey for her sharp eye and astute suggestions and for simply being a dream editor.

I'm extremely grateful to my parents, Ron and Jackie St. Jean, for giving me the priceless gifts of a happy childhood and a lifetime of unconditional love and support, and to Mehdi, Elianne and Anissa for making me ridiculously happy to wake up every morning. Merci beaucoup!

Trina St. Jean grew up in northern Alberta but later moved to pursue degrees in psychology and education. She also holds an MFA in Writing for Children and Young Adults from Vermont College. She now lives in Calgary, Alberta, where she teaches ESL and evades grizzlies in the nearby Rockies with her husband and two daughters. *Blank* is Trina's first novel. For more information, visit www.trinastjean.com.